Survive the Dungeon
Dead Dungeon Book One

Survive the Dungeon

Dead Dungeon Book One
S Mays
[Mailing List][1]
[Facebook][2]
[Website][3]
Cover art by: Alberto Besi
Cover typography: Plumstone Book Covers
© 2019 S Mays. All rights reserved.
This is a work of fiction. Names, characters, places, and incidents either are the products of the author's imagination or are used fictitiously. Any resemblance to actual persons, living or dead, businesses, companies, events, or locales is entirely coincidental.
F:2

---

1. https://www.subscribepage.com/SMaysSuperbTales

2. http://www.facebook.com/superbtales

3. http://www.s-mays.com

Dedication

For Aunt Patty.

Other Books by S Mays

https://www.s-mays.com/the-good-stuff.html

CHAPTER ONE
Awakening

Blinding pain wracked my body. Its intensity paralyzed me. I prayed for it to end, but my prayers went unanswered. The soothing embrace of unconsciousness followed.

So thirsty. So cold. I shivered. Opening my eyes, I found I was unable to see. For a terrifying second, I believed myself blind. The room I was in slowly faded into existence as my eyesight adjusted to the darkness.

I was in a rough-hewn cave. A sliver of light emanated from high above. I clambered to my feet and gasped as the room spun around me. I was forced to lean over and brace my hands against my knees in order to stay upright. The dizziness passed, but my head began to throb. I sat down on the unforgiving floor until the pain subsided.

"Hello?" I called out into the darkness. There was no sound other than my breathing. I stood again. What was the source of that light?

I moved across the room, observing the top of the cave as I went. There was a crack in the high ceiling, through which the light seeped through. At least I was close to the surface. How did I get here?

I tried to remember the last few hours but can't recall. In fact, I was unable to remember anything. My name. My last meal. Friends. Family.

My mouth was parched as if full of dust. My stomach ached. How long had I been here? I took stock of myself. I was wearing thin cloth pants held on by a cheap piece of twine. My lean body looked almost emaciated. I was covered in grit and dirt. The faint odor of alcohol lingered.

"Hello?" I shouted again, but this time my voice was directed at the crack. Something skittered in the darkness. After long moments without answer, I decided to inspect the room.

It was a round cave with no doorway or entrance. How had I come to be in such a place? Was I a prisoner?

I felt along the walls, hoping to find a clue. Nothing. Panic began to gnaw at my subconscious.

"Steady. I am here, so there must be an entrance. I did not spontaneously come to be in this place," I said to myself. My low voice clashed against the oppressive silence, but it reassured me. Again, there was the sound of claws against the stone as something moved outside of my range of vision. I froze. The sound ceased.

Straining my eyes, I scanned the room. Due to its circular nature, it was impossible to tell from where the sound originated.

I braced myself with my back against the wall. Whatever it was, it seemed to have left the room. I moved about, looking for the exit, but found none. *Something was in here.* Remaining silent, I listened and forced my eyes wider. Yet the darkest edges of the cave remained just out of sight. The thin beam of light from above was less than a flickering candle.

My stomach growled and I cursed at the sound. If something dangerous were close, my body would betray my position. Crouching low, I tried to prepare for whatever might come. Nothing happened. How had the creature exited?

Again, I explored my surroundings, but found no exit. Had it been my imagination? The oppressive darkness grew around me as if threatening to swallow me. No, the light was fading. Night must have been falling outside. Again, my stomach groaned. I swallowed my saliva several times, wishing it could provide some form of comfort to my empty belly, but soon it ran dry.

Sitting on the opposite side of the room from where the noise had emanated, I decided to conserve my energy. Had someone buried me in this pit? Why couldn't I remember?

Trembling, I curled into a ball in an attempt to maintain my body's warmth. My single wish was for the floor to somehow warm up from the heat I was generating, but it remained cold and unyielding. If anything, my body cooled against it. I put my hands down my undergarment to keep them warm. The cloth provided only moderate insulation. In the fading light, I could see it was a basic and functional garment, dull white and only moderately soiled.

I tried to remember a time when I was warm — a crackling fire, a comfortable bed, even a basic blanket. Nothing came to mind. The darkness closed in as I shivered myself to sleep.

The slender blade of light awoke me the following morning. After staring into complete darkness during the night, I felt like an old friend had returned. Again, my stomach roiled in protest. Feeling the need to relieve myself, I headed to a far corner of the cave. A small indention in the floor was just big enough to hold the urine. The act of urinating points out that despite my empty stomach, my bowels now required attention. I tried to remember the current location in relation to where I slept so that I won't stumble upon my waste later.

Licking my dry lips, I recalled stories of wanderers who were forced to drink their own urine in order to survive.

"Let's hope it doesn't come to that," I whispered. "Hello! Is anyone there?" I shouted toward the small crack in the ceiling. Each time I called out, I listened for minutes, hoping to hear a reply. Standing in the tiny beam of sunlight, I imagined it warming my body, although it was much too small to do much. I then noticed that the beam had moved several inches from when I had awakened. Perhaps it could be used as a rudimentary clock?

More grumbles of hunger. Could the cave contain mushrooms or moss that was edible? Despite the lack of memories about myself, it seemed my knowledge of general things remained. Plant names, rock types, months, math, science. Such rudimentary information remained, but no memories about myself.

Again, I inspected the cave, this time checking the walls and floors more thoroughly. After two more fruitless passes, I rested in my sleeping area. The only reward for my efforts was a small rock that had dislodged from a portion of the wall. What I needed was sustenance and escape, not a rock.

A human could survive without food for weeks, depending on their body composition. Looking at my lean frame, I estimated that I could perhaps go a week without food before I became too weak to move. The more pressing matter was dehydration. Already parched, I desperately needed water.

The cave walls were damp with moisture, but there was no trickle of water from an underground spring, which would have been a blessing. The condensation was merely a result of the cooler temperature in the cave.

Tentatively, my tongue probed the wall where a sheen of moisture had gathered. It tasted as well as I had expected, but the minute amount of moisture gathered seemed miraculous. If only I had a way to collect it. The damp edge of my undergarment brushed my leg. "Aha!"

Tearing off a small hand-sized piece of cloth, I swabbed the wall. In seconds, the cloth is saturated with water. Twisting it, a welcome trickle flowed into my eager mouth.

"Perhaps not enough to live off of, but enough to keep me alive for now," I muttered.

My sunlight friend faded away again, signaling nightfall. I lay back in my sleeping corner and listened. My muscles trembled from my explorations during the day. Was I really this weak? My estimation of a week's survival time might be incorrect. I had to escape this room.

CHAPTER TWO
Unexpected Visitor

The following day mimicked the first, except my hunger had grown. I considered the idea that perhaps I should remain still and not exhaust my energy reserves. By continually searching my surroundings, I would inevitably collapse from exhaustion.

The day passed without incident. I scoured the wall for precious water and slept when I could. The unforgiving stone floor was more akin to a torture device than a proper bed. Thinking back, I recalled sleeping in a ragged inn and complaining about it. What I wouldn't give for that bed now.

Yet, the rest of the memory was lost. I couldn't recall to where I traveled or why. The year and month of the trip were blocked from me. I could only recall parts of the incident. The feeling I was not alone on the trip nagged at me, but not a single face of a fellow traveler came to mind. It was infuriatingly frustrating.

Sitting in the dim darkness, I glanced at the sliver of light as it crawled across the room. The near total silence roared in my ears like a thundering herd of horses. A man could go mad in these conditions. At least in a prison, the inmates had each other to converse with. I think I would perish from lack of food before madness overtook me.

The idea of a prison returned to me. Rather, the feeling that I now resided in a dungeon or jail. This small cave appeared to be a natural phenomenon, but deep inside, I had the strange notion that I was being locked away and tortured by some unseen entity. Surely, someone had to have put me here.

Escape remained at the forefront of my thoughts, but how? There was no entrance or exit. How had I entered a room with no entrance? Had it been magic? A secret door? I felt as if I'd searched every inch of the walls and found no lever or button. Of course, if it was a dungeon or jail, it would make no sense to put the control mechanism on the interior of the cell. I started shouting again but stopped after a few seconds. It would most likely be a waste of precious energy.

Sitting back, I attempted to think of what had brought me here. I could remember mundane knowledge about the world, but not anything specifically related to my own life. Friends, family, lovers...nothing. Bits and pieces of scenes and events but nothing that would help me remember who I was. It was as if my life had been reduced to a dream. I knew people were there, but they remained just outside of my vision, or blurred. I focused harder but was rewarded with a splitting headache.

Although I could not recall any experience working with magic, I had a suspicion my predicament was due to magical forces. The impenetrable cave, the specifically blocked memories — it was unnatural.

The pain in my abdomen reminded me of more immediate needs. The trickle of water I scrounged from the wall barely satisfied the ever-encroaching thirst, but my hunger grew. After a wasted day, I turned in for bed.

MY HUNGER PANGS AWOKE me the following morning. I relieved myself in the far corner – or at least I attempted to relieve myself. Only a trickle emerged. The smell had become more noticeable, but my one concern was filling my empty gut. The glaring beam of light appeared more intense today. With nothing else to do, I moved under the light and stared up at the hole. I longed to see just a glimpse of the blue sky. Instead, I saw a small wriggling dot high above. For long minutes, my brain attempted to make sense of it. A fly. There was a fly in the chamber, buzzing close to the ceiling. Perhaps it had made its way through the small opening, drawn by the smell. A vision of my desiccated corpse, crawling with maggots and flies, flashed into my mind.

I noticed several more in the chamber. The small bugs could provide meager sustenance, but as disease carriers, they were too risky to eat.

Several hours later, my light friend had diminished. The room grew dark. The faint sound of thunder shook the cave. Moments later, a drip of water through the hole soon turned into a steady stream. I rushed to it, allowing it to wash over my body. It was cold but invigorating. I opened my mouth to drink as much as I could. It felt like the most marvelous gift I'd ever received. I scrubbed my scalp and cleansed my body of the filth I'd accumulated.

It had been a mistake. I became nauseated for a moment. I'd drunk too much, and my empty stomach felt as if it was going to heave it back upon the floor. Inhaling slowly, I forced the feeling away through sheer willpower.

I lay back down in my corner and rested, shivering involuntarily. It had probably been foolish to soak myself in the cool water, considering the temperature of the cave. At the very least, I should have removed my undergarments and pants, which now squished beneath my bottom. I sighed and curled into a ball, attempting to gather some warmth. My eyes grew heavy and I soon drifted off, but a familiar noise awakened me.

The skittering sound chilled me to my core. It was as if bone scraped against stone. Something sniffed the air, searching. Fumbling in the low, orange light, I located my rock and stood. Moving against the wall, I scanned the room fearfully. I then located the intruder on the far side of chamber.

It was about the size of a large dog. As it moved about, something trailed it. It took a moment before I realized it was a long tail. It sniffed about in the corner that served as a makeshift latrine. Disgusted, I realized it was rooting about in my waste. How had it entered the cave? It was roughly one third my own size, and I would have noticed a hole that large. The vague outline of the creature looked like something I'd seen before, perhaps in a book.

A ratzgor. A large rodent with a long whip-like tail that was covered in thin, bladed bone protrusions. Each was sharp enough to cut through cured leather. The creature had teeth like a canine, built to shred flesh. Boney disks protruded around its shoulders and head to protect it from predators. Against an unarmed man, it could prove deadly. I stood motionless and held my breath as it went about its disgusting meal. I was curious to see how it had entered the cave. If the hole proved large enough, perhaps I could find freedom once it left.

A single drop of water from the hole above dashed that plan. I stiffened as it splashed into the puddle that was the remnant of the earlier shower. The beast jerked around and hissed at the noise. It then looked up and noticed me. It hissed louder and crouched low into an attack stance.

"Whoa...no need for that, boy. Just finish your meal and be on your way," I said in a calming voice. I tried to keep a neutral, non-threatening posture, but the rodent cautiously approached as if analyzing me. I felt foolish being terrified of something that I outweighed twice over, but its two-inch claws, tail, and fangs beat out my feet, fists, and rock. In the wild, I could perhaps find a long, heavy stick for defense, but in this dark, enclosed space, one strike from any of its natural weapons could mean death.

Ratzgors' preferred method of attack was slashing at their foe with their tail, attempting to catch an artery. They then retreated until their foe was weakened from blood loss. At this point, they moved in for the kill. Unfortunately, I was already weakened from lack of food, and this animal seemed to be able to sense it.

Now close enough, it tensed and spun around quickly. The deadly tail cracked against the wall beside me. I hustled to the side as it spun about again. For a moment, I considered throwing my rock, but if I missed, I'd have nothing else to defend myself. It lashed out three more times. Each time, I barely skirted to the side. Keeping myself against the wall helped halt the tail's momentum. It seemed the creature's attacks weren't very precise, but one lucky hit could result in a mortal wound.

I'd kept ahead of its attacks, but I was tiring. Each small dodge sapped my limited strength. A desperation took hold of me. While this creature was physically superior to me at the moment, I was more intelligent. I would not be killed by a mere rat. The next time it attacked, I dove over the tail and brought the rock down on the massive rodent's back with all my strength. In a fortunate turn of events, I heard its spine crack. It squealed in pain and attempted to spin around again, but its tail and hind legs no longer functioned.

I rolled away, stood, and watched the injured creature crawl forward with only its front legs. It hissed and whined alternatively, now afraid of me. I watched it go and slowly followed but kept my distance. If it was merely stunned, it could regain the use of its lower body and attack again.

It reached the far wall and proceeded through it. I blinked several times and moved closer as it dragged itself through what appeared to be solid stone. As the tip of its tail was about to disappear, I reached through and felt no resistance. A secret passage? I was sure I had investigated this very spot. I did not know what awaited on the other side, but I was desperate to escape the cave. Sucking in my breath, I wriggled through just as the ratzgor's limp tail passed through.

CHAPTER THREE
Small Victory

I emerged into utter darkness. No friendly sunlight slivers existed on this side of the wall. I could hear the ratzgor's hissing and ragged breathing to my right. I considered allowing it to escape, but it could return if it recovered. Inching forward, I estimated its position. My leg merely brushed the creature's tail and I gasped as I felt a thin cut open. I moved ahead and brought my rock down repeatedly on the beast's back and head. It screamed and hissed until the life was beaten from it. I felt a twinge of sorrow, but exhaustion then overcame me. Killing the intruder had nearly sapped the rest of my limited energy.

As I lay on the floor, gasping for breath, a faint noise gave me pause. Holding my breath, I listened. A scratching sound echoed farther down the passage. Could it be another ratzgor or perhaps a worse predator?

I inched down the wall, feeling along the walls and floor as I went. After a dozen feet, my panic grew. I should have located the passage by now. Could I have missed it somehow? No, I was positive it was close. How did the beast pass through? On a hunch, I crept back and fumbled in the darkness, careful to avoid the deadly tail until I felt the rear leg of the massive rodent. Dragging it across the floor, I felt along the wall as I went. My hand passed through the wall. A magic doorway? That made sense in a wizard's tower or sanctum but not a cave.

I crawled through, feet first, and dragged the creature as I went. For whatever reason, the creature could pass through freely, but I could not — unless I was touching it. Once through, I let go, allowing it to block the entrance. It looked as if the wall had swallowed half of the creature. It seemed the magic door was somehow keyed to the creature. I decided to keep it lodged in the door, as I did not want to become trapped again.

If something else wandered outside, hopefully the carcass of the ratzgor would deter it, and if that failed, the body should at least help block the entrance for now.

The ratzgor chose that exact moment to release its bowels and bladder. Disgusted, I retreated. "Fantastic. If I want to exit, I'll have to crawl through it," I muttered to myself.

Exhausted, I retreated to my corner to rest. I noticed my small sanctuary was at the farthest point from the hidden passage. Had the choice of location been pure luck? If I had been closer, the creature might have wandered in and killed me as I slept.

The thought of sleep caused my eyes to grow heavy. Weary from my battle, I succumbed and drifted off.

Jerking awake, I lashed out at an unseen enemy. The cave was quiet. The small beam of light was just awakening for the day. It looked as if he would be strong and helpful today. The fetid smell of the ratzgor caused me to gag. To my surprise, I did not feel the urge to relieve myself this morning. Instead, I moved to inspect the rodent.

It had stiffened overnight. The pain in my stomach reminded me I hadn't eaten in days. Was it possible to eat such a creature under these circumstances?

While they fed on carrion, waste, and small creatures, these particular rodents were almost totally immune to disease. In fact, many bought ratzgor spleens and livers on the black market because of their reputation for creating a strong immune system. Still, the thought of eating raw meat from such a disgusting creature repulsed me. Again, my stomach growled. Perhaps a small bit of flesh from its flank...

How could I remove the tough hide? My rock was too dull. If only I had a keen blade. I looked at the cut on my leg, then the beast's tail. It was just as sharp in death as it was in life. Carefully working it back and forth, the stiffness faded, allowing me to maneuver it.

I twisted it around and pressed one of the barbed bone blades against the beast's rear leg. Using it as a makeshift saw, I eventually cut through the tough hide. I could see the bloody muscle underneath. My mouth watered, although I was repulsed by the idea of eating the raw flesh of the lowly rodent. I held up a sliver of quivering, juicy flesh to my sunlight friend and we inspected it together.

"I've heard people in some kingdoms delight in eating raw meat. Today, I'll try my hand at it," I said to the light before sliding the raw flesh into my mouth. I swallowed it whole. My stomach cramped almost immediately, doubling me over. I gasped in pain. A smaller piece would have been a wiser choice.

Once the pain subsided, I sawed off a few more tiny pieces and ate them at a slower pace. A few times, I visited the wall and soaked my rag for moisture. I looked at the hole in the ceiling and wished it would provide the beautiful stream of water again. "I do not wish to offend, Sunbeam," I said.

After devouring a few small slices of flesh, I sat against the wall and thought of the hidden doorway and the space beyond.

The area outside felt different from the small cave. The floor was smooth, and the walls were angular — as if built by man. If it was a structure, it would logically have an entrance and exit. The path to freedom obviously did not lie in the cave I occupied. I would have to venture out if I wanted to survive, but without tools, a torch, or weapons, the area could be dangerous.

I looked again at the barbed tail. The tip of it was essentially all bone. At least twelve inches of it. If I took a bit of hide from the beast and wrapped it around the base of the tail bone, I would have a makeshift shiv. I moved back to the creature and inspected it. The tail was too tough to rip apart by hand, but I could use the claws to slice through the tendons.

Working the tail around, I sawed through the largest toe on the rear foot until it broke loose. Carefully feeling along the tail, I found an indention below the flesh, indicating where the end bone connected to the rest of the tail. It was gruesome work, made difficult by the blood covering my hands, but eventually I cut the tip free.

Using the toe, I cut several strips of hide from the torso of the ratzgor and wrapped them around the tail until I could grip it in my hand without fear of being cut by one of the ridges.

Exhausted, I sat back in my corner and analyzed my makeshift weapon.

It was far deadlier than my rock and gave me a few more inches of reach. The gory toe had proved to be a useful tool as well. What else could I salvage from the creature? Perhaps a small bit of clothing or a blanket? I knew very little of tanning. Removing the hide for my handle had been work enough. My limited energy would be better spent finding an exit, but the light had begun to dim again. My escape would have to wait until morning.

CHAPTER FOUR
Leaving the Nest

I awoke the next morning feeling stronger and refreshed. My stomach had resumed its regular complaints, but eating any more of the rodent meat would be risky after so much time had passed. I sopped up as much water as I could from the damp walls and gulped the precious droplets. The vision of a bucket of ice-cold water from a stream materialized in my mind. It was now worth more than all the gold in the world. I envisioned a piece of bread. My determination increased. "I will not die here," I whispered to myself.

Hooking the toe cutter into my undergarment, I gripped my makeshift shank tightly in my right hand. The homemade leather handle had stiffened overnight. Looking up, I noticed the light was dim today. "Are you sad that I'm leaving?" I asked aloud before chuckling to myself. I needed my sunlight friend far more than he needed me.

I shoved the corpse of the ratzgor aside and slid through mystical doorway in the wall. Of course, its waste smeared over my body as I predicted, but nothing was going to stop me from leaving this place.

Outside, I waited long moments for my eyes to adjust to the darkness, but it was as I feared: there was no light. I felt along the edge of the wall, this time opposite from the way I had gone while pursuing the giant rodent.

Stale and dusty air filled my lungs. Whereas the cave was damp and moist, this new area felt old and dry. It made no logical sense. Was the doorway a portal spell as well as a hidden door? Off in the distance, a clattering caused me to pause. It was impossible to tell from which way the sound had come. I continued along the wall, exploring as I went. Perhaps I could find a torch or a lantern. The wall felt like worked stone in opposition to the unyielding natural walls of the cave I had just left. I was in a man-made structure of some type.

The wall fell away as my hand traced the angled indentions of a doorway. The familiar hallmark of civilization eased my concerns. If I was trapped within a building, there must be an exit.

I crept into the room and almost immediately found a torch on the wall. My luck was turning. I continued searching the room, looking for anything of use, such as a striker or a magical igniter. Discovering a shelf, I felt along the top of it. It collapsed, sending its contents crashing to the floor. The rotted wood disintegrated in my hand.

A shriek echoed from down the hallways, setting the hair on the back of my neck on end. The sound had been decidedly inhuman. I moved back to the doorway, relieved when I felt the edge of a door on the opposite side. Pulling it, I cringed as the well-rusted hinges cried out in protest. The door resisted my effort, but my sudden surge in strength due to fear granted me the ability to close it. The latch no longer worked, but it wedged shut tight. In my mad scramble to close the door, I lost my shiv and accidentally kicked it with my foot. I leaned against the door to hold it. I prayed that my body weight would be enough.

Thankfully, the door's wood felt much sturdier than the crumbling shelf. A moment later, something outside the door snorted. I held my breath and listened. It sniffed the air and shuffled past the door a few times before silence followed. I couldn't tell if it was gone.

Releasing my body from against the door, I began to sit up when I felt the door push inward slightly. Stiffening, I tried to keep my position without allowing it to open. If I pushed too hard and closed the small gap between the door and the frame, whatever was on the other side would know I was here. It pushed harder, causing the wood to creak ominously. My left foot slid an inch across the dusty floor.

The pressure ceased. The unknown creature grunted several times before footsteps led me to believe it had finally departed. I collapsed on the floor, breathing and sweating heavily. I waited several minutes before feeling around for my weapon. It had slid into a nearby wall. With it in hand, I felt a bit of my confidence return.

I now had a torch, a bone shiv, and my small razor claw, but my easy exit had been stymied by the fact that something else lurked in the darkness. Judging by the force it had applied to the door, it was fairly strong. It did not seem to fear the dark, however, so it possibly had a type of night vision. Whatever it was, I should avoid it at all costs. I couldn't afford to spare the energy, and even a small wound could become infected in this unsanitary environment.

I continued inspecting the room — this time with more caution to avoid any more loud noises. I discovered a withered cloth...something. Perhaps it had been a shirt at one point. As it crumbled in my hands, I felt several insects race up my arm. I brushed them aside while lamenting the loss of a possible piece of clothing. This new area was not quite as cold and damp as the previous cave, but it was far from comfortable.

I discovered a rotting table and gently probed its surface. A brittle parchment brushed my hand, breaking into several pieces. I also felt what I assumed was an ink well, now dry.

After exploring the small storage room, I was disappointed that I found nothing more of value. A sword, blanket, or anything would have been encouraging, but the torch would have to do for now. Now I would need a way to ignite it.

Lifting on the edge of the door, I slowly swung it open just enough to slip by. Returning to my sanctuary, I felt as if I'd let my sunbeam friend down. "Sorry, I must return to rest."

I rehydrated from the water on the wall and inspected the torch. It looked as if it would function, if I could find an ignition source. If I were lucky, it would prove to be a magically enhanced torch which could last for a day or more, but such advancement in magic was uncommon in the distant past, and I had no way of knowing how old this structure was.

A low buzzing noise came from the rotting corpse of the ratzgor. I moved to inspect it and was repulsed by the decaying odors. Dozens of flies now flitted around the corpse. Movement on the rear flank caused me to lean down to investigate. Maggots. The wounds I'd created were now crawling with hundreds of maggots. The vile white larvae writhed in unison, devouring the rotting flesh. I fought back a wave of nausea.

I moved back to my corner and contemplated shoving the corpse out into the hall outside. The flies and maggots would only grow worse, as would the smell. The light was now fading. Sunbeam returned home after a long day of work. Exhausted, I too decided to conserve my energy. Tomorrow would be the day I found the exit and left this place.

CHAPTER FIVE
It's Not That Easy

Again, my stomach awoke before my brain. It seemed to now be in charge of my body. The tiny bits of meat I'd ingested were long digested. The previous day's excitement had exhausted what little energy I had.

The buzzing from the far side of the room had increased in volume. I could visibly see some of the flies crossing through Sunbeam. "Sorry for the mess," I apologized.

I found myself envious of the small, writhing, disgusting larvae. Imagine being that size, with enough food to fill your belly a thousand times over. The rodent's carcass could feed the maggots for weeks, even if they multiplied hundreds of times. It seemed unfair that I should starve while they feasted.

A repulsive idea formed. Must I go hungry? I inched closer, while attempting to hold my breath. There were now many more maggots than yesterday. Could I eat these writhing, disgusting creatures? I knew it was just as unsafe as eating the raw flesh of the rodent, but while the ratzgor had natural immunities to disease and infection, the maggots did not. It was too risky. If I had a way to cook them, it would be safer. I eyed my torch. If only there were some way to light it.

If I could produce enough friction with two pieces of wood, it was possible, but the rotted wood in the storage room would break apart, and I didn't want to risk dismantling the door. The dusty, dry wood from the broken shelves might burn, but I'd need a way to generate heat. If I had a flint and steel, I could perhaps start a small fire.

"Do you know where I could find any fire-making tools?" I asked Sunbeam. Right now, Sunbeam must be shining down on thousands of people, all eating, making food, smithing, hunting. It was ironic that he also had a presence in this cave while also observing the entirety of the world. Sunbeam was necessary for life on the planet, but down here, he could only provide me with a small bit of assistance. If only I had discovered something useful in the storeroom.

"Wait, you may yet help, my friend," I whispered as I grabbed my weapons and excitedly made my way to the exit. I leaned through the passage and listened for a moment before exiting and making my way back to the room. I soon returned to my sanctuary with my prizes.

I held the inkwell up to the light. The dried ink inside flaked away easily. I used bits of wood from the shelf to clean out the insides until clear glass remained. I broke up a bit of the shelving into small dried pieces at the point of the floor where Sunbeam rested. Holding up the inkwell, I could see the glass on the bottom was curved slightly, like the lenses of eyeglasses. I moved the glass container up and down, attempting to focus the light into a point on the wood. It was only partially successful, because the top of the container blocked too much light from reaching the curved base. I'd have to shatter it and remove the top.

Grabbing my rock, I placed the inkwell on the floor near the edge of the room. I would not want to step on any shards later, considering I was barefoot. "Please, Theala, let this work," I prayed. I brought the rock down and the glass shattered. The base remained intact with jagged shards from the walls of the inkwell remaining. It was almost perfect.

Returning to the pile of tinder, I again focused the beam of light. The available energy was now much greater than before. The focal point was not as precise as I'd wanted, but it would have to do. My hands shook as I attempted to hold the beam in one spot. Sweat dripped from my forehead, dampening several places on the wood. "Light, damned wood," I cursed. A faint wisp of smoke curled upward from the pile. At that moment, the light dimmed.

"Not now!" I said. A cloud must have passed over. After five minutes, I began to worry that the clouds had filled the sky and the light would not return, but then the rays intensified back to their former levels. I quickly moved back into position, although I had to move the wood slightly to get the beam back into the same spot. It took less time to call forth the smoke. A minute later, a red ember appeared. "Yes…" I whispered. Blowing gently on the ember, it glowed brighter. My hope grew as well.

Fire! A flicker of flame emerged in the darkness. I felt as if I had created life itself. I almost fumbled my makeshift lens as I moved to encourage the small flame. I sprinkled a few more flakes of desiccated wood from the shelves on it until it was twice as large. After a few minutes, it had grown into a tiny, respectable fire. I'd never felt such beautiful heat. It was like a thousand sunrises on my face at once.

As the fire grew, I went back and forth to the storage room, gathering more and more wood. I noticed the smoke rose up to the high ceiling, disappearing into the various cracks and crevices that I assumed led to the surface. Sunbeam was lost in a haze as the smoke exited through his doorway. I observed the situation for a moment longer, making sure the smoke would not fill the room and asphyxiate me. Satisfied, I curled up near the fire and reveled in its blessed heat until I was sufficiently warmed. I then moved to the corpse of the ratzgor and removed several of the disgusting maggots with a piece of wood.

Holding the edge of the wood over the small fire, the maggots sizzled instantly. After a few seconds over the fire, each one burst open like corn kernels. The display turned my stomach, but the smell of cooked meat overrode my disgust. Popping one of the worms into my mouth, I considered the flavor before eating the rest. It would be generous to say they were pleasant, but in my weakened and hungry state, I ate several dozen of them. I was far from full, but the hunger pains subsided again.

I gathered more water in my cloth and consumed the droplets by the fire. "What I wouldn't give for a flagon of mead," I whispered as the earthy water barely dampened my mouth. Noticing several maggots had fallen from my wood plank onto the floor, I wondered if the wriggling carrion feeders felt pain. They'd dropped down beside the fire and writhed due to their proximity. I moved to crush them and put them out of their misery when I noticed something peculiar. Two of them had doubled in size. Were they inflating from internal gases due to the heat? I watched for seconds more, unsure if they were about to burst.

Instead, they doubled in size, then doubled again. In seconds, they were now as big as my fist. "What sorcery is this?" I gasped. I searched for my rock, but before I could locate it, they had grown to the size of the ratzgor. Seconds later, two giant maggots only slightly smaller than myself squirmed blindly, thrashing about. One snuffed out part of the fire as it rolled over it. They began to edge toward me, but I quickly moved as far away as possible. They hesitated before turning toward the rodent's corpse. I wasn't sure how these unusual maggots sensed their food or prey, but it seemed to be by smell.

Each spat a spray of black bile upon the dead rodent's body. It sizzled as its flesh dissolved and formed rivulets on the stone floor. The giant maggots slurped the liquidated flesh.

"By the gods," I whispered. I grabbed my shiv and made my way around them, attempting to reach the exit, but one of them turned and shot a stream of the powerful acid in front of me. I hopped back and grabbed the torch from the floor. I lunged toward the fire, touching the tip of the torch to it. The torch roared to life.

I jabbed it in the face of the maggot that had attacked me, causing it to scream and roll about. It shot another spray of acid, which coated its brother maggot. The second one dissolved so quickly, it split in half. Apparently, their external flesh was not immune to their own acid.

The blinded maggot continued to thrash about before I brought the shiv down into what I assumed was its brain. Its translucent-white body housed several dark internal shapes which were its organs. Puncturing several, I then jumped back before it could spray its acid again. However, it seemed to have run dry, as it no longer attacked. In moments, it was dead.

Panting, I collapsed on the floor. What had caused such a transformation in what appeared to be simple maggots? Had it been the flesh of the ratzgor? Then why had the others remained normal size for so long? Something had triggered them to grow. Their proximity to the heat, perhaps? My curiosity forced me to seek the answer.

I rebuilt the remaining fire and experimented for an hour with several maggots. In the end, I concluded that it wasn't just the heat that had trigged their rapid growth, but any severe pain would. If I fatally sliced one and left it alone, minutes later, it began to grow. Dipping part of one in some of the black acid also resulted in rapid growth. If it was killed fast enough, such as when I cooked them over the fire, they remained nearly the same size. I hadn't noticed, but even then, some of them had started to increase their size, although fractionally. As time went on, they grew faster if left alone. A fascinating defense mechanism. Was it limited to the maggots in this cave? Regardless, it was obviously magic-related. No creature could grow to such a size without proper sustenance, and so quickly.

I eyed the rat carcass. My mind now regarded it as a trap waiting to be sprung. If something happened to the maggots on its body while I slept, the cave would be infested with the monstrosities in minutes. There would be nowhere to run.

Shortly after, I observed my torch had not lost much of its mass during the past hour. As I suspected, it was likewise magicked. Judging by how much material remained, it was a powerful enchantment. It could possibly last several days or longer.

Feeling stronger after my unappealing meal, I decided there was no better time to set out in search of the exit. My chamber had become much more dangerous. I kicked the fire away from the corpse, gathered my torch, shiv, and razor in preparation to leave.

I slithered through the small false section of the wall and inspected the hallway. It was formed of man-made stone with wood braces and metal. I felt relieved to see a reminder of human civilization. Moving down the hall, I paused to revisit the storage room. Glancing around inside, I found nothing else of use.

The next room was also used for storage. Its door had rotted from its hinges and fallen to the side. I found another torch inside and tucked it through my flimsy belt. At the end of the hall, a large metal door awaited. A small, barred window in the middle of door invited a peek, but I could not see into the darkness beyond. I pushed against it, but it was locked.

I turned around and froze. Two dozen feet away, the outline of a small figure stood motionless against the limit of my torch's light. It appeared to be a child, judging by its frame and size. Yet my instincts told me this was no human. I waited to see what it would do.

It slowly backed away, disappearing from the light of my torch. "Wait!" I shouted. "Is there a way out of this place?" It ran down the hall. I cautiously followed, but it disappeared.

"Blast it," I snarled. Continuing, I peered into several rooms. These appeared to be more storage rooms, but a few contained rotted beds that had decayed under layers of dust and spiderwebs. I entered one room to test the soundness of a bed, only to have it crumble under my finger's pressure. It would have been marvelous to have a good night's sleep on a proper bed under a warm blanket, but it seemed that would have to wait until I escaped.

None of the rooms contained a window or doorway out. After exploring the rooms and walking a fair distance down the hall, another large, metal door blocked my way. Strangely enough, I had not run into the small figure. Were there other invisible doors?

Sliding the torch through the bars on the door, the darkness beyond resisted my efforts to see any further. I turned to head back, only to barely avoid a sword strike. The blade struck the metal door with a clang.

I leapt to the side and barely blocked the sword's reversed swing with the torch. Embers flew from the torch as it shook in my hand. I knocked the sword away and thrust the torch forward, hoping to blind my attacker. That's when I saw its face.

Light blue slimy skin reflected the torch's light. A large, domed head held only a single eye which swiveled on a stalk like a crustacean. The creature's mouth proved to be its most disgusting feature. Instead of teeth, its black gums held dozens of wriggling tendrils that looked exactly like massive earthworms.

"A psuthal!" I whispered. The diminutive creatures lived deep under the ground, usually in clans. They possessed a rudimentary level of intelligence and were able to create basic weapons, clothing, and armor. They never ventured to the surface. Their single eye provided enhanced vision in even the darkest places, and their mouth tendrils were able to burrow into most creatures to suck out sustenance. This one had apparently thought to stab me in the back while I was distracted.

"Back, creature!" I shouted while swinging my torch. I brought my shiv up toward the creature's midsection, but it blocked it with a small buckler. It slashed again with the sword, causing me to jump backward and crash into the door.

It pressed in for the kill, but I twisted at the last moment, bringing my bone weapon up to block its sword just as I lashed out with the torch. The blistering-hot tip seared the psuthal's single eye. It shrieked and dropped the sword just as I swirled around and buried the shiv in its belly. It gasped and doubled over, shrieking in pain.

I quickly retrieved the sword and brought it across the small humanoid's throat, silencing it forever. It fell forward onto the ground and spasmed for a minute while its dark, red blood oozed out around it.

I inspected the sword. In the hands of the psuthal, its proportions looked to be a normal-sized sword, but it was a short sword. Minor bits of rust flaked spots on the blade, but it still remained a potent weapon. Squatting down, I swept the torch's light across the corpse. It wore small bits of piecemeal armor and a belt with several pouches on it. I unbuckled the belt. The creature had cut several more notches in the belt to make it fit its small form. Using the regular notches, I found it to be a bit loose on my malnourished frame, but it did fit. Certainly, it was better than my cord.

The pouch on the left contained a piece of moldy cheese. I swear, it might as well have been roast leg of lamb. I bit into it with fervor. Tears almost filled my eyes at the sharp and delicious flavor.

A loop on the right back of the belt held a waterskin. I unstrapped it, opened the flap, and sniffed the contents. A tentative sip proved it contained only water. I'd hoped for wine, but the flavorless liquid managed to slake my ever-present thirst in a manner that wall drippings never could. I took one more small bite of cheese and a small sip before stowing my feast for later. I then searched the second pouch. After a bit of effort, I fished out a small metallic object.

An iron key.

CHAPTER SIX
Wrong Way

Beyond the massive steel door laid a stairway descending into darkness. I turned and trekked back to the far end of the hall. My goal was sunlight, not to travel deeper into this unknown facility.

With trepidation, I tried the key in the next door. The lock proved difficult, but in the end, it relented. The door groaned on its ancient, rusty hinges. Opening it just enough to slip through, I cautiously inspected this new area.

Dozens of prison cells lined both sides of the walls. Dust, spiderwebs, and corrosion covered the bars. Looking into the first cell, I gasped. Two skeletons occupied the cell. One sat with his back against the wall, and the other lay in bed. Each cell contained the bones of prisoners in positions that looked strangely serene. Almost as if they were resting...or waiting. I became more uneasy as I traveled down the hall.

The next door was identical to the first two. Looking through the barred window, I gasped. There, far down the hall, was my friend Sunbeam. He poured in through a small opening. Was it a window? It felt as if he were beckoning me to join him.

My hand shook as I slid the key into the lock. I prayed that it would open. The lock would not turn. The key fit, but the lock felt as if it were fused shut. I twisted the key so hard my fingers throbbed. It would not budge.

"Blast it!" I shouted as I slammed my fists against the door. I unleashed my frustration on the door, kicking it several times and hacking at it with the rusty sword. A glow arose from where the sword had struck last. Curious, I prodded the spot with the sword again. The light expanded across the door, painting it in a bright, purple glow made of tiny hexagons.

"Magic," I muttered. A noise nearby raised the hackles on my neck. "No..." I whispered. Several soft clacks, clicks, and clinks emanated from a cell a dozen feet down the hall and on the left. I took several quiet steps back toward the open door at the end of the hall, keeping my back against the right wall. A bony hand emerged from the darkness, gripping the cell bars, followed shortly by a skull bereft of its lower jaw. The empty eye sockets looked first left then right before coming to rest on me. As I inched down the wall, the skull slowly rotated to follow my movement.

As I passed the cell, I noticed the other prisoner inside now stood as if waiting. In each cell I passed, the occupants were no longer at rest. In fact, they looked as if they were about to attack. A bony hand reached through the bars behind me and grabbed my throat. One might expect decrepit skeletons to be weak, but whatever now animated these had imbued them with great strength and durability. I twisted away, leaving deep red abrasions on my neck. As one, the entire cell block moved to intercept me.

I dashed for the rear door, avoiding the lunging arms and hands that now clawed at me. The sound of metal grinding on metal followed behind me. Looking back, I saw each door swing outward. One on the left, the right, then left, as if synchronized. The skeletons poured forth, their bony feet sliding and scampering across the hard, stone floor. I quickened my pace, driven by fear. Would I end up as an occupant of one of these cells, or would I be torn to pieces on the spot? I had to keep ahead of the doors as they opened, or I'd be overwhelmed.

The opening doors passed me before I could escape the jail. I shoved by several skeletons, slipping through their grip. Bringing my sword down hard on the neck vertebrae of one just as it emerged, I wondered if they could be incapacitated. The sword crushed the ancient bones more than it cut, decapitating the skeleton. I felt relieved when its body tumbled forward a few feet before falling to its knees. I leapt over the disabled skeleton and raced onward. Several behind me tripped over their companion, forming a jumble of writhing and interlocked bones. Their movements were slow and unsure, just as a man's was when he first awoke in the morn.

Now through the door, I struggled to shut it. At the last moment, it closed. I fumbled with the key, barely locking it as several arms grasped at me through the barred window. Bones smashed and clawed at the heavy metal, but the door held. I picked up the torch and limped away, the pain of fatigue suddenly piercing my side as I gasped for breath. Dust-infused sweat trickled into my eyes.

Turning to look back, I saw the skeletons frantically scratching and clawing through the bars, now in a frenzy. It was as if it took a moment for them to fully awaken. Whereas before, they were lethargic; now they had a speed and fervor that belied their lack of muscle and tissue. The clamor generated by the bony horrors echoed through the halls. I wondered what other creatures could hear the racket. Suddenly, I became aware of a pain on my shoulder.

Setting the torch in a nearby sconce, I surveyed the damage. In the heat of the moment, I hadn't noticed, but several of the undead terrors had managed to grab or strike me. Angry red furrows crossed my shoulder where their bony talons had raked. My back and thighs held several bruises, and of course my neck felt inflamed. I decided I would recuperate in the cave.

The noise instantly stopped. I turned once again and found no trace of the skeletons. Had they returned to their long slumber? Had whatever spell that animated them before worn off? My curiosity piqued, I waited to see if the situation had defused.

Something flew out from between the bars of the window, landing near my feet with a *clack*. I grabbed the torch from the wall and cautiously waved it near the object. It was the hand of one of the skeletons. Another object landed close by — an arm. Several more pieces followed. Were they cleaning out their den? Tossing away the one I had destroyed?

The hand leapt to life and began crawling toward the arm. It rotated around and backed up to the wrist and instantly connected as if they were two magnets brought close to one another. In a panic, I waved the torch around and saw that a shin bone now had a foot attached.

"No..." I whispered, backing away from the eerie sight. I turned and ran down the hall, my mind racing. Should I hide? Lock myself in a room and hope the door held? Then what? The skeletons could wait for all eternity. I would be dead in days.

I paused and considered turning back. Perhaps it would be better to attack it before it had reformed. Yet how could I destroy it with the tools at my disposal? Any limbs severed would just reattach. I would need to grind it to bits to incapacitate it, but even then, there was no guarantee that whatever dark magic animated it could not repair it again.

Continuing, I soon reached the stairway down. The sheer darkness sent a chill through me. There had to be another way. My mind flashed an image of the glowing window and the promise of freedom. A repetitive clacking sound caught my attention. It was growing louder. It was coming.

I stepped through the door and strained to shut it from the other side. Once shut, I locked it with the key. The clacking grew louder. I looked up at the barred window. The skeleton must have had the help of its compatriots in order to send all its parts through the first window. It would not be able to do that by itself, but what prevented the others from sending more through the first door? There could be a small army within the hour.

I held the torch up to the window, allowing my eyes to rise just enough to see through the bottom edge. The skeleton slowly limped into sight, missing several parts, including a foot. Most notably, it lacked a head. Of course, certain bones were too large to fit through the barred window.

I watched the misshapen jumble of bones feel its way around the walls. It looked as if a child had been given instructions to rebuild a medical skeleton. Its general shape was correct, but many parts were attached incorrectly. It seemed less of a threat now.

But more could follow. Even without a head or pelvis, the skeletons could kill. My sanctuary was lost. I turned and took the next step down.

CHAPTER SEVEN
Level Two

At the base of the steps, another locked door barred my path. My heart sank. What if the key did not work? I'd be trapped in the stairwell with an ever-growing threat lurking above. Fortunately, the lock turned, and the door opened. In fact, it opened too easily. It made no noise and swung open with no effort, as if someone — or something — had maintained it and kept it oiled.

I felt vulnerable as I stepped into the new area, my torch illuminating me in the darkness. It had taken so much effort to ignite that I refused to douse it. Gripping my sword tighter, I moved forward. I'd either find another exit or a means to destroy the skeletons and the magical barrier above.

This floor had seen more traffic. Dust did not cover every surface like above. The first door I encountered was in good shape. There was no way it was as old as the ones above. The door was made of thick, dense wood, with another barred window at head level. It appeared to be a cell. Visibility was limited, but a disgusting, rank odor emanated from inside. The smell was similar to a rotting corpse combined with a pig farm.

The entire hall contained similar doors. Each door was locked, and my key did not fit. I slipped down the hall, aware of the fact that if I was attacked, my only exit was back to the stairs leading up. I would be cornered.

At the end of the hall of holding cells, I came to another door on my left. Peering in, I was surprised to see a faint illumination, although it was dim and far off. Something moved under the light, but it was too far to see clearly. I thought I heard a faint grunting or sniffing noise from deep inside the room. It looked as if it contained dozens of large objects, resembling furniture or machinery of some type. No, this was a torture chamber.

My brain at last made out the shapes in the darkness. An iron maiden...a bloodfuser...other terrifying devices meant to rend flesh, destroy minds, and worse. I stepped away. Behind me, another hallway led off into darkness. The fragrant smells of a delicious, cooked meal immediately wafted through the hall. My stomach growled and my mouth salivated. Looking over my shoulder to make sure it was safe, I hurried down the shorter hallway.

To my left, an open door led to a large bunk that looked to be currently inhabited, but the occupant was not present. Glowing magic orbs illuminated the room in a dim light.

Clothes laid strewn on the floor. Foul odors assaulted my nostrils, presumably from the clothing. A gargantuan bed, larger than any I'd ever seen, sat in the corner. A large desk, bookshelf, and other living amenities decorated the room. The man who lived in this room must have been a small giant. I opened a drawer and pulled out a plain shirt. I longed for some clothing of my own, but this would have been akin to wearing a child's sheet. Across the hall, another dark room beckoned to me, but the delicious smell of food was coming from the third door, to the left of that one.

Cautiously entering the room, I realized it was a makeshift kitchen. Racks of pots and pans hung from chains from the ceiling. A stove burned in the corner and a large pot bubbled on top. Various crates and boxes of cooking ingredients, vegetables, and flavorings were stacked upon each other throughout the room. I immediately grabbed an apple and devoured it in seconds. A carrot atop a wooden table disappeared into my waiting belly. I found the fragrance from the pot to be too alluring. I set my torch on the edge of a table and weighed it down with a box of herbs.

Grabbing a small, basic wooden bowl and a spoon, I lifted the ladle out and dished up a large helping. It appeared to be a stew. Carrots, celery, and potatoes swam in thick, brownish gravy-like sauce. It even contained bits of thick meat.

I tentatively tasted it. My eyes grew wide. It may have been a result of my starvation, but my mind told me whoever had cooked this was a culinary genius. I shoveled in several more spoonfuls until the spoon clattered against an empty bowl. I looked around on the floor, expecting to see the stew that I must have dropped. No, I'd devoured it so fast, it only seemed like it had vanished. My now-smaller stomach groaned in protest, but it had complained for days about the lack of food. It was now going to accept this gift, whether it had capacity or not. I scooped up another ladle and attacked my now-full bowl.

My belly felt as if it would split down the middle, like a ripe melon dropped on a cobblestone road. I regretted eating so much. Locating a basin of water, I cleaned my dishes and placed them back from where I'd found them. A nearby pitcher contained…wine. Despite my body's protests, I gulped down several ounces of the delicious fluid before putting it back. I stowed another apple and carrot in a pouch in my belt. Just then, a loud clank rang out. Whoever lived here must be returning from the torture room.

Although it pained me to lose my reliable source of light, I doused my torch in the water basin and looked about for a hiding spot. If the clothes fit him well, I would not want to meet whoever approached.

The kitchen presented no safe hiding spots, so I dashed across the hall. I could now hear footsteps growing closer. It sounded as if the person approaching wore thick boots with tough soles or perhaps wooden clogs. I quickly slid under the giant bed, careful that my sword did not strike anything and give away my position.

Louder the footsteps grew until I saw the thick legs clomp into view. Trotters. This person had pig-like trotters in place of feet. However, his legs were thick and muscular, not fat. He could probably cave in a man's chest with one kick from those powerful legs.

He walked into the kitchen, snorting and grumbling. He held something over his shoulder, which he carelessly tossed onto the table. Something metallic slid free and clanged down hard on the thick wood, resulting in a round item rolling off the edge of the table and to the floor. It continued out of the kitchen and into the dim light cast into the hallway from the room I occupied. I gasped at the grisly object.

An old woman's frightened face stared back at me, her eyes wide with terror. The beast of a man cursed and stomped into the hall to retrieve it. Bending down, I caught a clear view of the monstrosity. He stood close to seven feet tall. His stout body and large gut may have given a person the sense he was weak and fat, but signs like the veins in his forearms indicated his tremendous strength. He'd tossed the body of the woman on the table as if she were a small chicken although she must have weighed at least a hundred and fifty pounds.

His face and head were a combination of human and swine. A piggish nose protruded from his face, elongated ears flopped as he moved, and inhuman beady eyes regarded the severed head on the floor with disgust. I slowly retreated farther into the shadows of the bed, fearful that he'd catch sight of me as he bent over to retrieve the decapitated head. He jerked it up by the hair and returned to the kitchen, tossing it into a barrel of waste in the corner. A loud *chunk* followed as he began chopping the body to bits.

"Stew ain't no good without more meat," he grumbled.

I raised my hands to my mouth, barely able to contain the bile that rose into my throat. My stomach grumbled as my digestive juices reacted to the new stress resulting from the revelation that I'd just participated in cannibalism...and enjoyed it.

Sampling a portion of the stew, he grunted in satisfaction before leaving the kitchen and returning to the other room. When he returned, the pig-man slid a chamber pot under the bed before getting undressed. Tossing his filthy trousers onto the floor, I noticed his belt was a thick leather tool belt which contained various metal utensils and...a set of keys.

He flopped onto the bed above. The underside of the bed sagged dangerously low with his weight upon it, almost touching my chest. A moment later, a tremendous snore filled the room.

The chamber pot exacerbated my nausea, so I was relieved when I could silently crawl out from under the bed. Once out, I observed the bestial man for a moment, making sure he was deep in slumber before retrieving the keyring from his belt, which laid on the floor with his tangled pants. Surely one of the dozens of keys would open the exit. If this floor contained an exit to the outside, it would either have to be in the room across the hall, the torture chamber, or the hall that extended past the torture chamber.

I started to leave the room, but grabbed one of the giant, thin shirts before leaving. The cloth could prove useful. I rolled it up and slid it into my belt, looping it around on top so it wouldn't slide free.

Ducking into the kitchen, I grabbed a small sack and stuffed several bits of food into it. I made every conscious effort to avoid looking at the poor woman's body parts that now littered the table. I hadn't noticed the blood-stained floor before due to my hunger and focus on obtaining food. The pitcher of wine caught my eye. After two fast swigs, I left. I then spotted a true prize beside the stove: a firesparker.

The small, metallic object was the size of a large man's thumb. At one end of the magical device, a cap protected a dual tip. Once the cap flipped open, a small flame appeared between the two small prongs, suspended in midair. The useful gadgets cost half a year's wages for most laborers, but worth every gold. I slipped the device into a pouch and continued to the room beside the kitchen. Even if it did not contain an exit, maybe I'd find something else useful.

The magical globes in the room were dimmer than the ones in the pig-man's bedroom. It took time for my eyes to adjust. Once they had, I again had to fight the urge to vomit. The tortured visages of dozens of heads stared out blankly from where they were mounted on the walls. Some were humans, others were not. Several of them had torsos attached to their heads, their arms fading back into the wooden plaques as if absorbed into the wall.

I turned to leave when I heard a low voice to my right. A female scalax's head sat atop a partial torso that was mounted to a wooden plaque. Her pained eyes pleaded with me. Slowly, I backed away toward the door as her eyes followed me.

"Do not go," she whispered.

I blinked several times, unsure if I was dreaming. Surely this was nightmare.

"You must kill him," she whispered. Pain filled her voice. Whatever process had cut her into pieces and kept her body alive, despite being on display, apparently tortured her even in death.

"H-how are you alive?" I asked.

"Kill the pig. Release us. I beseech you," she said. Tears traveled down the jeweled scales that covered her face.

A loud snort from across the hall filled my heart with fear. I wouldn't end up like one of these unfortunate souls.

"I-I'm sorry..." I said as I backed through the door. Her eyes glistened as I slunk back into the hall.

Terrified, I ran toward the end of the passage. Even if I couldn't get out, I had to get away from that foul creature. There was no chance of beating him with my dull, rusty sword. He looked to be at least double, if not triple, my weight. Even if I wasn't half-starved, I wouldn't want to face him without a heavy crossbow.

At the intersection, the metal door to the torture chamber blocked my way forward. The holding cells were to the left. I could only hope the doorway out was to the right. Once outside, I'd notify the authorities of this hellhole. After two steps, a sound behind me caused me to pause. It had come from the torture chamber. Moving to the door, I grabbed the bars and put my ear closer. Someone inside was crying.

I looked through the window but could not locate the source of the sobbing. Glancing over my shoulder, I imagined the giant beast racing down the hall, meat cleaver in his hand high above his head. "I'll send back help," I whispered to myself, letting go of the door. Ashamed at my cowardice, I turned to leave.

"H-hello?" a soft voice called out from inside. Puzzled, I wondered how she knew I was here. My voice couldn't have carried that far.

"Is there anyone there?" the unseen woman whispered louder.

Blast it. At this rate, she might start screaming and awaken the pig-man. My guilty conscience won out over common sense. After trying several keys, I found the one that opened the door and slipped inside, locking it behind me. Unless he had a spare key, at least we'd be safe inside if he awoke.

Making my way past the grisly machines, I worked my way toward the dim light. Why were there so many devices? At least fifty people could be tortured at the same time using all manner of unspeakable methods. After making my way past a large wooden "X" with manacles at the top and bottom, the dim light illuminated a naked woman who was stretched out upon a rack.

She had wavy blonde hair, which cascaded down across her large breasts. She looked to be about five and half foot tall, with long, slender legs and a curvy waist. Her pale blue eyes begged for help. She was beautiful.

"Thank Pilon that you happened by," she breathed. "Quickly — unshackle me so we can escape."

"Escape? You know the way out of this godforsaken place?" I asked as I stepped forward to assist her.

"Just set me free, and we can escape together!" she said, the volume of her voice rising. "I've been trapped in this place for weeks."

"Quiet — if he hears you, we are both doomed," I said. I paused as I looked at the empty floor in front of me. The devices in the room seemed to be arranged in a symmetrical pattern, as if the organizer wanted a certain amount of room between each one. Each machine placed in a certain spot to achieve a certain function. The floor in front of me looked oddly out of place, as if something should have been there, but wasn't. Had a machine been removed to be repaired?

"What are you doing? Come help me!" she practically shouted.

Sidestepping the suspicious area, I moved to her side and inspected her bonds.

"Who are you? An explorer?" she asked as I tried to find a key to fit the locks that held her wrists.

"I-I don't know who I am. I can't recall," I said as the latch popped open, freeing her arms. I moved down to the bottom of the machine to undo her ankles. My gaze drifted up and beheld her vulnerable form stretched out before me. She sat up and rubbed her wrists and smiled.

"You're my savior, and that's all that matters," she said. She swung down from the machine and fell to her knees.

"Can you walk?" I asked. She reached up, indicating she needed help. Leaning down, I looped my arm around her waist and helped her to her feet. She leaned into me, seemingly grateful for the assistance.

"I feel so weak," she whispered.

There was no way I could carry her. My strength had mostly returned, but even if I was at full strength, she'd be too heavy. One meal wasn't going to fix that.

"Just give me...a moment. My joints haven't moved in days," she said as she flexed each limb. "Okay, I think I'm, ready."

We moved back toward the door, but she suddenly turned and went back toward a table near the wall.

"Wait, I left my —" she said.

"No!" I shouted, shoving her to the side. A large metal box dropped from the ceiling where she'd just been a moment ago, slamming into the stone with a loud *clang*. It was the spot my instincts had told me earlier to avoid.

I helped her to her feet. "How did you know that was there?" she asked.

"I don't understand how you did *not* know it was there. You've been here for weeks, but didn't think there was something suspicious about that spot?" I replied. After a moment, the box rose to the ceiling again. I supposed that if it contained nothing, it automatically reset to its original position. Bending down, I located a plate in the floor which triggered it. I wasn't sure if it was a trap, or if the machine was stored on the ceiling to save space. Looking up, I noticed several more devices around the room hanging closely to the ceiling.

She retrieved a necklace from the table and dusted herself off. "He never came that way," she explained.

"We can only pray he slept through that," I said. "Are there any clothes or items here that you know of?"

She pointed to the workbenches around the room. "Only instruments of torture."

The devices indeed looked painful and menacing, but nothing appeared to be better than my sword for defense. I spied a grindstone in the corner, but we needed to flee before the pig-man returned.

Moving toward the door, I motioned for her to follow. "We need to move. Follow me. What is your name?"

"My name is Zarah. What's yours?" she asked.

I started to speak before I remembered that I did not know my name. "I'm…I don't recall."

"You don't know your own name?"

I frowned. "No, I lost my memory somehow."

She looked at me suspiciously and asked, "And you know a way out of this place?"

"I was hoping that you did. I don't, but damned if I'll be here when he returns. Have you seen any other prisoners?" I asked as we neared the door.

"There was a man a few days ago and an old woman…"

"Yes, I saw her fate. We must hurry or we will share it," I said as I fumbled in the dark for the correct key. I should have separated it or marked it somehow. My hands trembled as I tried each key. "Damned if it wasn't the last one," I said as I slid the key into the lock and breathed a sigh of relief.

"Wot wuz that noise?" a voiced boomed from the other side of the door. The heavy clomp of hoofed feet echoed down the hall.

We looked at each other in fear.

"Too late," Zarah whispered.

CHAPTER EIGHT
Torturous

Backing away slowly from the door, we waited to see if the pig-man would leave.

A heavy fist rapped against the metal door. "Oy, I know I heard someone in there! Come out before I kick this door in!"

I looked to Zarah, my heart racing in my chest. "Does he have another key?"

"I don't know."

The blows against the door became more violent. Dust shook from the edges of the door where the hinges attached to the stone. Cracks began to appear.

"We need to find a place to —" I began, before the door crashed to the floor. We both froze as the monster regarded us with surprise.

"What are ya doing in here?" he asked, looking at Zarah. His gaze fell on me. "Oh, ya found yerself a boyfriend? He's a good lookin' one. We'll put 'em in the face peeler and see what kind o' mask we can make, eh?"

I pointed to the far side of the room. "Go that way!" He would be unable to follow both of us. To my relief, he chose me as his target.

"You're the little shit who done stole my keys," he said as he stomped around a giant wooden wheel.

"I'm just trying to find my way out of this place," I said, as I moved around a metal pyramid that came up to my waist.

He stepped over the pyramid and drew closer. "There's only one way out fer the likes of you."

I brandished my sword. "Just let the two of us go."

He chuckled as he gingerly moved a large coffin out of his path. "The two of you? The girl ain't goin' nowhere. She belongs here."

I couldn't see Zarah. I hoped she'd made her way to safety. Now I could focus on the monster in front of me without worrying about her.

"Ya goin' to dance the whole night?" he asked.

"I wager you'll get tired before I do," I said as I leapt over a bench.

He slapped his hand against his large, bloated gut. "Naw, you're lookin' a bit tired and malnourished. I might be a stout fellow, but I got energy to spare."

He was right. If I'd been well-fed and rested, it would be different. I was panting already, and my knees felt weak. I needed to change strategies.

Purposely stumbling, I allowed him to gain ground on me. He lunged forward to grab me, but I slashed upward, catching him in the shoulder with my sword. He fell back, holding the slight wound.

He lifted his hand, inspected the damage, then turned to me and smiled. "Fer that, I'll put ya in the fuser and graft yer head on a goat."

The damage inflicted by my sword had been minimal. It was due to a combination of the dull blade and his thick, porcine hide.

I ran back toward the benches which held a variety of instruments of torture. Although they looked menacing, they did not have enough reach to work as proper weapons. Grabbing a chain, I whirled it around and accidentally knocked over a large, oil-filled lantern.

"Careful, fool!" the beast man shouted. He moved to a wall and unwound a large chain that had a manacle attached to one end. "Looks like mine's bigger'n yours."

He swung it over his shoulder, before lashing it forward and bringing it down perilously close to my foot. Sparks erupted where it struck the stone floor. One hit from that would mean the end of the fight.

Reaching across the table, I grabbed the lantern and moved around the monster, barely dodging another attack from his chain.

"Ya look kinda tough and stringy, but a few days in the stew can soften up most anyone," he said as he stepped forward.

I checked over my shoulder and gathered my bearings before slowly inching sideways toward the door.

The pig-man followed my gaze and leapt sideways, blocking the path. "Oh, no ya don't! I ain't chasin' ya up and down the halls all night."

I tossed the lantern at him. It shattered on the floor, splashing oil around his feet.

He jerked back as if he'd expected flames to engulf him, but the flame went out on impact. He smiled for a moment before becoming angry again. "Oy, that was my best lantern, ya dumb bastard! That's goin' to cost ya a few days in the ball vice." He stepped forward, spinning his chain again.

Instead of retreating, I dashed forward, slashing frantically with my sword. Surprised, he backed up several steps. One blow nicked his right wrist, while a second sliced deep into his finger. He tried to right himself, but my attack left him off balance. His hard trotters slipped and skidded on the oil-covered stones as if he were on ice. One foot struck a certain plate on the floor.

"You little —" he said as he slipped backward. He looked up just in time to see the large metal box descending upon him. Despite his size, it enveloped him completely. The clangs of his fists on the metal rang out across the dungeon. I wondered if the contraption would hold him.

"What would happen if you turned that crank on the side?" Zarah asked as she appeared at my side.

I jumped at the sound of her voice. "What — what are you doing here? I told you to run."

"I couldn't get out, so I came back to help," she said. She pointed at the handle on the side of the machine and nodded.

The beast banged louder on the walls of the device. "What are ya doin' out there? Let me out of here, ya bastard!"

I looked once more at Zarah before grabbing the crank that she'd pointed out. I wound it around once.

"No! Stop!" The creature's tone had changed to utter fear.

I cranked it again, resulting in a loud scream from the prisoner. I wound it several more times. At some point, the yelling and screaming had turned to unintelligible gurgles and whimpering. The crank stopped, apparently at its limit.

Zarah moved to a lever on the wall and pulled it down. "Let's inspect your handiwork."

The crank on the side of the box rolled backward until it had reset to its original position. The chain became taut and the box slowly rose back to the ceiling. I gasped at the sight before us.

A quivering square roughly one-fourth the size of the pigman now lay on the floor. It was as if he'd been compressed into a perfect cube. His flatted face stared out from the top of the cube, while the outlines of his folded arms, legs and body were visible on the sides. His eyes darted back and forth as his mouth tried to move.

"By the gods..." I whispered.

Zarah chuckled, sauntering over to the cube before sitting down on it. She crossed her legs demurely. "He makes a better seat than a man."

"But how...how is he still alive? He should be dead."

"Many of these devices are magical. They can keep a victim alive even after being tortured or transformed. He wasn't jesting when he said he could put your head on a goat's body."

She seemed far too calm about the grotesque form underneath her rear. Although, she must have felt a huge relief that her torment was over. Maybe it was her way of revenge for the torment she'd suffered.

Walking to a workbench, I found a small knife, which I used on the huge shirt that I'd tucked into my belt. In moments, I'd created a poncho and a ragged skirt for Zarah. I tossed the ratzgor's nail and shank onto the table and slid the knife into my belt. A coiled rope caught my attention and I added it to my pilfered items. That could prove useful in many situations.

She stood from her grotesque seat and clothed herself. "My, aren't you the gentleman? Most men would force me to go nude."

I had to admit: the sight of her voluptuous body had been enjoyable, but we had more immediate concerns.

"It's just until we can either find a way out of this place or find you better garments," I said. "We should look through this floor for useful items. But first..." Moving to the grindstone, I sharped my sword and removed as much rust as possible. The edges were razor-sharp once I was done.

We looked throughout the torture room but found nothing of interest. The rancid smell of rotting flesh warned us away from a few locked devices.

"What about him?" I asked, pointing at the wobbling cubed pig-man. "What if he regains his normal form?"

Zarah bent down and lifted the cube. It seemed the device not only reduced his mass, but also his weight. She placed him in an iron maiden, closing the door and locking the latch on it. "There. If he transforms back, he'll have a nasty surprise." She wiped her hands on her skirt and smiled mischievously.

We stepped over the broken door and walked to the bedroom. Zarah went to the kitchen and returned with a cleaver, the pitcher of wine, and a bag of food. We finished off the last of the wine and filled my container with water.

Upon closer inspection, the bed smelled almost as bad as the chamber pot underneath it. It was also swarming with bedbugs. We threw the dirty clothes in the floor into the bed and emptied all of the dressers onto the floor, creating a makeshift bed of clothing and blankets. Strangely enough, despite the disgusting room, the articles in his drawers seemed to be professionally washed. Compared to the cold, unforgiving stone floor above, this makeshift bed looked like paradise.

We ate a few of the vegetables and fruits. I cut off a portion of cloth, soaked it in water and began to clean some of my wounds. None were serious, but infection could set in.

Zarah saw me attempting to reach a spot on my back. She took the cloth from me and motioned for me to turn around. "Allow me."

I laid flat on my stomach and heard her gasp.

"By the gods, were you a slave?" she asked.

"I don't know what you're talking about," I said as I turned over slightly.

"Your back has almost a dozen scars from the lash. They look perhaps a few months old."

I reached around and managed to find the edge of one raised scar. "I...didn't realize they were there. I don't know what that's from." I thought back, trying to pull forth any memory. Had I been a prisoner? Was that why I was in this place?

She gently cleaned several spots on my back. Despite the tenderness of the bruises and cuts, it felt good. "How did you gain these fresh wounds? They resemble handprints in some places."

"On the floor above, I was attacked by reanimated skeletons. I barely escaped with my life."

She began to knead several areas on my back and motioned for me to lie down flat again. "A remarkable tale. Undead guards, a half-man, half-pig torturer with magical devices. What sort of place do you suppose this is?"

"A place I plan to leave as soon as possible. If you didn't see the skeletons for yourself, how did you come to be here?"

"I don't recall, exactly. I believe I was kidnapped. I worked at an inn. I saw what I thought was a child crying in an alley late in the night. I went to investigate and woke up here," she said as she massaged my lower back.

My vision blurred as exhaustion overwhelmed me. Yawning, I asked, "What...did you do at the inn?"

"I was a bard, of course. Would you care for a song?"

I struggled to keep my eyes open. "That...would be wonderful."

Zarah's voice dropped to a whisper and steadily rose as she wove a tale about an ancient forgotten kingdom and its rise to power. Her song ebbed and flowed, soothing my senses one second before stirring my imagination the next. Between her caresses and her serenade, I felt like a babe in his mother's arms.

"So lovely..." I whispered as I drifted off.

CHAPTER NINE
Company

For the first time since I could remember, I awoke in supreme comfort. The soft bedding meant my poor bottom and back no longer had to suffer the cold, stone floor of the cave. Heaps of clothing provided a warmth that soothed my bones and joints. I felt as if I were in a cocoon — and did not wish to leave — but nature called.

Crawling out from the makeshift bed, I was astonished to see the beautiful young woman that slept beside me. It took me a moment to shake the fog from my mind. I looked around the room and remembered. This wasn't a dream — it was a nightmare. The room across the hall contained deceased trophies of torture victims. The aroma that stirred my hunger was that of human stew.

I retrieved the chamber pot and relieved myself. Part of me wanted to crawl back into bed and feel Zarah's warmth against my body. It would be foolish to linger longer than necessary. The skeletons could find their way down, or some other creature could wander in from perhaps a hidden passage.

Grabbing a torch, I lit it and entered the trophy room. Cautiously, I inspected each one. I touched the scalax woman's face with the back of my hand. It was cold and hard.

"Hello?" I whispered. She did not move. It seemed whatever magic had kept some of them alive had ended with the pigman's defeat. Part of me felt sorrow at the deaths, but it was mercy.

"What are these?" Zarah asked, causing me to jump. That was the second time she'd snuck up on me. I wondered if she hadn't also been a thief in addition to a bard.

"Trophies from his victims. A few of them were alive before we defeated him. This place is full of foul magics."

She made a sour face as she looked over the room. "Disgusting. Do you think this would have been my fate if you hadn't interfered?"

I thought about the cube machine and the other devices I'd seen in the torture chamber. "If you'd met your demise on the rack, it would have been more merciful."

We returned to the bedroom. "We should take some of this cloth for bedding," I said. I began cutting the shirts into sheets.

Zarah watched me work before holding out her hand. "Allow me your blade for a moment." She then sliced up a piece of cloth and wrapped it around my waist. "If I had some thread, I could make you something better."

Looking down, I wasn't sure if what she'd done was an improvement. Now it looked as if I were wearing a short skirt.

Zarah noticed my embarrassment. "Oh, you look rather fetching. Perhaps you could dance for me the next time I perform."

Blushing, I ignored her comment and rolled up several sheets into a roll and wound the rope around it. Padding two strands of the rope with cloth, I then looped the straps around my back.

Zarah nodded her approval. "Very creative. Where'd you learn such crafts?"

I thought for a moment, but the memories eluded me. "I...don't know."

"You're still unable to remember your past? Your mother, father...friends? Where you are from?"

Focusing, I attempted to draw forth personal memories. It was as if a black wall blocked that history, but not my understanding of zoology, botany, weapon use, or other knowledge.

"No. I can't recall such things."

"I've heard that memory may be triggered by certain fragrances, music, or sights," she said.

I frowned. "I don't think the aromas and sights of this place will elicit anything. At least I hope I've never been to such a place before."

We ate a light breakfast, inspected the room one more time, and made our way to the exit. I considered taking one of the magical light orbs, but they were firmly attached to their bases and tended to be very brittle. We took a right in front of the torture chamber. More cells lined the hall. Curious as to their contents, I opened one with one of the keys on the keyring.

The dingy cell contained a pile of straw and a nearly full bucket that smelled similarly to the pig-man's chamber pot. I didn't know if it contained an old meal or bodily wastes, but we hastily exited.

SURVIVE THE DUNGEON

"Were you ever kept in one of these cells?" I asked Zarah.

"No," she said abruptly. It seemed she didn't want to dwell on her captivity, so I did not press the matter.

After a short walk, another metal door similar to the previous ones between the levels barred our path. One of the steel keys on the ring opened it with a click. I held the torch out as we descended the stairs. The key fit the next door that awaited at the bottom of the steps.

"Quietly," I whispered as I opened the door a sliver while holding the torch back. I let my eyes adjust to the darkness but was unable to see anything. No, I could see a light at the end of the hall. It grew brighter as I watched.

I closed the door. "Someone is approaching!" I doused the torch with the makeshift covering Zarah had made for me, singeing it. She did not look amused.

Low voices became audible. I held up two fingers as I made out two separate voices. Then a third spoke.

"Next game, I deal. G'blog cheatin.'"

"You cheat worse than G'blog. I cut own dick off before let you deal."

"I deal. You cheat, too."

"You waste all your silver playin' cards, but not me."

"Too good for us? Yout think you better'n rest of us?"

"Said no such thing. You want die?"

The voices trailed off to our left.

Zarah placed her hand on my shoulder. "Who do you suppose they were?"

"Guards on patrol. Their nasally voices and dialect make me think they may be goblins."

A look of disgust crossed her face. "Nasty creatures. At least they shouldn't present too much of a problem for us."

"One or two may not, but it sounds like there could be a large group. They can be formidable fighters with the right training and equipment." I lit the torch with the firesparker.

We inched out of the doorway and crept down the hall. My hope was that if another group spotted us in the distance, they'd think we were one of their comrades. At that moment, a faint glow appeared around the corner ahead. We ducked into a nearby storage room and hid behind some empty barrels and doused the torch again. The door opened and an orange-colored goblin entered.

He grumbled to himself as he grabbed a barrel on the far side of the storage room, laying it down so it would roll. "Don't see why I get mead. Got it last time. Not fair at all. I kill him if talks to me that way." He turned his back to us.

Sensing an opportunity, I slipped behind him and grabbed his mouth as I put my knife to his neck. He struggled briefly, but I was stronger. In fact, I seemed much stronger than I had been. The combat with the pig-man and the rest and meal above must have reinvigorated my waning muscles.

"Don't say a word unless you want to die," I whispered. "Nod if you agree." Slowly, he moved his head up and down.

"How many of you are there?"

He held up four gnarled fingers.

"Four?"

He shook his head in the negative.

"Forty?"

He nodded in the affirmative. I was dumbfounded. It was not possible to beat forty goblins with just the two of us. Perhaps clad in full battle plate and with enchanted weaponry or with a full party of warriors...

"I'm going to take my hand away. Do not do anything rash if you wish to live. Do not turn around or move." He nodded again.

I removed my hand but kept a tight grip on the knife, pressing it harder against his neck. "What is this place?"

"It — it's dungeon."

"I know that, you blasted fool. What is it called? Where is it located?"

"I know not what mean. It just dungeon. It been here since I can remember."

Frustrated, I tried a different line of questioning. "How do we get out? How are supplies delivered here?"

"A disappearing light. Goblin goes in light, comes back with supplies."

This sounded promising. "A teleporter? Is that what you mean?"

The goblin shrugged. "I don't know what tela-portor is."

"Nevermind. Where is the light?"

"In party room. Where goblins play games and drink."

"How many are in there now?"

The goblin's voice became excited. "Most. Most stay in room. Play cards, darts, fight, drink. Except guards. Guards must guard until it's their turn to go to party room. Unless time for sleep. Then Chief yells and all goblins go to their bunks for night. Chief doesn't like noise all night."

I didn't like the sound of this "Chief."

"Is there another way out?"

The goblin nodded again. "Door down to next floor or door up. But only supposed to take supplies and leave on other side of doors, not go down or up."

I turned to look at Zarah. "Sounds like we just have to wait until they go to bed, then we can sneak in and use the teleporter."

The goblin turned his head. "Who talk to?" His eyes grew wide and he opened his mouth as if he were about to yell. Zarah darted forward and planted her cleaver directly in his forehead. A splash of blood blinded my left eye. The goblin flailed his hands at the handle, but his coordination no longer functioned properly due to the damage to his brain.

Zarah grabbed the handle firmly and kicked the goblin away. Blood gushed from the wound, leaving him senseless as his life seeped away. He gibbered for a few seconds before dying.

I stared at Zarah in shock. "Why...did you do that?"

"He was about to scream. You should have slit his throat instead of staring at my cleavage."

"I wasn't —" I said as I looked back at the body of the goblin. It seemed cruel to kill him after he'd cooperated, but what was the alternative? Tie him up and hope the guards did not hear his muffled cries? Now we had to figure out what to do with the body. If he'd been sent here to retrieve mead, it was only logical someone would come to see why there was a delay.

I then had an idea. I poured some of the mead out of one of the small barrels while taking a few large gulps for myself. Zarah joined in. Soon, the small barrel was almost empty. Unlike the huge barrels that lined the room, this one held perhaps several pitchers. While the flavor left a lot to be desired after thirsting for days, it might as well have been from a king's brewery. I doused the goblin's body with the last quarter of the alcohol, then laid his body down so it appeared he'd passed out. I then sent the barrel beside his hand. The entire room reeked.

We then set up two barrels near the door, forming a hiding spot on either side of the door.

I whispered over to Zarah, "We'll ambush the next one that comes in."

"You intend to kill forty goblins in this manner?" she asked.

"Thirty-nine now," I said.

She shook her head. "This plan is doomed to failure."

We waited for what seemed like an eternity. My eyes grew heavy as time passed. Perhaps I'd taken a few too many sips of mead. Just as I'd almost nodded off, the sound of heavy footsteps caused me to snap awake. The door opened, revealing a much larger goblin than the previous one. This one was almost the size of a man.

The large, brown goblin paused two steps into the room and snorted. "What doin', Fleck? That my mead you drink'? Stab your eye if it is!" He stomped over to the one named Fleck and kicked his leg hard.

"Wake up! I wait fer that barrel and you drink it up. Get up, I say!" he shouted louder.

He paused, as if listening. "Fleck?" he said as he bent over his comrade. Dashing forward, I thrust my sword into his back, up through his spleen and other organs just as I brought my dagger down on his neck. He turned about, his body jerking the weapons from my hands.

I looked at my weaponless hands in surprise just as he faced me. Not knowing what else to do, I brought my right fist into his jaw, which caused him to stagger back. I jabbed with my left, catching him directly in the nose. He toppled over Fleck and landed on his back. The knife and sword erupted from his front simultaneously. He quivered for several minutes before his life ebbed away.

Zarah stepped forward and admired the gruesome scene. "Nicely done!"

I rolled the larger goblin over and retrieved my weapons. It took considerable effort to pull the sword loose. Panting, I hopped up onto a barrel to rest. "Only...thirty-eight more to go."

"I believe this big one looks similar in size to you," Zarah said.

It took me a moment to realize what she meant. I jumped down and removed his shirt and pants. The woven-cloth pants were loose in the waist with splatters of blood near the top but were much thicker than the ones I wore. The shirt dripped blood on the front and back and had puncture holes from the stab wounds. I tossed it away. Once the blood dried, it would be stiff and uncomfortable, and I did not want the goblin's blood coating my body.

It was amazing how much more secure a layer of thick cloth made one feel.

"I notice you kept your old undergarment on," Zarah said.

I pointed to the naked goblin. "You'll also notice he wasn't wearing anything under these pants. I'd prefer not to catch anything from his nether regions."

Zarah laughed. It was an infectious laugh, full of hearty mirth. A laugh one would expect of a bard who had spent her life entertaining cheering crowds. "A wise decision."

We set up in our positions, but no other goblins entered.

My eyes felt heavy, but I refused to sleep. "I feel as if it must be very late at night. What do you think?"

Zarah yawned. "I agree. Should we see if they've gone to bed?"

"Perhaps I should go alone. It will be more difficult to hide two people if we are caught in a compromising situation."

Zarah stood. "No, you're not leaving me here alone. If this trend continues, the next goblin will be even larger."

I smiled and peeked out of the door, then motioned for her to follow.

We cautiously explored the floor. Down several passages, we found the barracks, but we chose to keep our distance. Even from this range, a cacophony of snores practically vibrated the walls. We retraced our steps. Looking to the left, I saw the fading light of a patrol.

"Not all of them are asleep," I whispered. Judging by how quickly the light faded, we'd have perhaps fifteen minutes until they returned.

After a few more moments, we stumbled up a large room at the center of the floor. A fire burned low in a massive fireplace on the right wall. A huge banquet table sat in the center of the room. Overturned tankards, cards, darts, battered chairs, trash, old food, and pools of liquid littered the room.

"Goblins aren't known for their cleanliness," I said as we explored the room.

Zarah peered over a small puddle of liquid and grimaced. "I've seen better manners from Mangorian barbarians."

Roaches and other insects skittered across the food remains. Rats dashed from the light back into the shadows. I scanned the room, looking for anything to indicate a teleporter. In the far corner of the room, a few crates and barrels were stacked against the walls, but the corner itself was bare. "There."

Zarah moved to the corner area. "Bastards are apparently too lazy to take their supplies to the storerooms."

"Are you familiar with these magical constructs?" I asked.

"They can be dangerous — or so I've heard. They can be attuned to certain items, which act like a key, or to individuals. If the wrong person uses it, it could fail to work or..."

"What?"

"It could even rip them apart."

I grabbed an empty bottle from the floor. "We'll test it with this." I rolled it toward the empty square. Upon entering the area, a dazzling blue flash illuminated the area, accompanied by a loud thrum. The vacuum created pulled air past us, creating a light breeze.

I smiled at Zarah. "I'll go first and step back through for you. If there are enemies on the other side, it could be dangerous." I took a step toward, sword and torch at the ready.

Zarah stepped between me and the magical area. "Wait. That proves nothing. It was an inanimate object. We should test it with a live subject to be sure it's safe."

Puzzled by her sudden concern when freedom was mere inches away, I grabbed her shoulders. "I'm sure it will be fine. They've obviously been using it to bring supplies in. Someone has to enter it to cart the items away."

SURVIVE THE DUNGEON

I started to move past her, but she grabbed me and pulled me close. "At least let me give you a kiss for good luck," she whispered as she brought her soft, delicate lips to mine. Surprised at first, it took only a moment for me to succumb to the gentle embrace. I closed my eyes as I moved my arms around her back. A strange sound and flash of light ended the moment.

I guided her away from the teleporter and looked about. "What was that?"

Zarah looked dazed but snapped out of it. "I don't know. Perhaps the teleporter reset?"

Grabbing a tankard, I rolled it into the square. Nothing happened. I tentatively reached forward before stepping in. "Blast it! It's not working anymore!"

Zarah frowned. "Perhaps it has to have time to recharge or can only be used once a day?"

The thought that I'd wasted our one escape chance on an empty bottle both frustrated and terrified me. I looked around the room. "Wait, that fireplace needs to vent the smoke, which would lead to the outside."

We doused the fire with the leftover tankards of ale and mead. Holding my torch up the shaft, I was dismayed to see a heavy, metal grate bolted into the stonework.

"Someone's coming!" Zarah whispered.

We dove under the table and pulled several chairs close.

"Why fire out?" A medium-sized brown goblin said as three of them entered the room. They wore leather armor and carried a variety of weapons.

A dark green goblin hit the smallest one on the arm. "I told put log on it last time we pass!"

"I-I did! It low but burning last time."

The brown goblin slapped the small one in the back of the head. "You lie. Let next shift handle it. Time for sleep." The two larger ones took a swig from one of the small barrels then led the smaller one away.

"Should we try and kill them in their sleep?" Zarah asked.

I shook my head. "I doubt we'd manage to assassinate thirty-eight goblins before one of them called out to the others or before we were discovered by a patrol. We could hide in a storeroom then try the teleporter again tomorrow."

"They'll look for their comrades at some point. Perhaps the chief would have the key to the lower floor?" Zarah suggested.

"How do you know there is another level?"

She shrugged. "It just seems...logical."

"Nothing about this place is logical. But you have a point. We may not be able to kill all of the goblins in one fell swoop, but killing their leader is another matter."

"As long as he doesn't follow the same pattern we've seen so far. It seems the larger the goblin, the more power they hold over the others," she said.

"How much bigger can they get?" I asked.

CHAPTER TEN
Tribal

Once the patrol passed, we followed at a safe distance behind, searching for the chief's room. After several dead ends, we located a long hall that we assumed housed the goblin's leader. We readied our weapons.

"You keep watch out while I eliminate him," I whispered.

Zarah held up her meat cleaver. "I feel as if I'm least-suited for combat." She paused and looked me over. "You're scared."

"Of course I'm scared. I'm in an enemy lair about to confront an unknown threat. I'm not an idiot."

She leaned in close and whispered a song in my ear. Despite the low volume of her voice, she managed to sing it beautifully. The song was of heroic deeds and knights vanquishing their enemies. The triumph of good over evil.

I felt stronger. My hands stopped trembling. "How did you do that?"

She smiled. "There is magic in song if you know where to find it. It can control minds, emotions, and hearts."

"You're no ordinary bard."

She pushed me toward the door. "And you'd best hurry before he hears us chatting away."

I entered the open door to find a massive study. A massive, ornate bed rested on the far side of the room. Again, magical orbs provided a low light, equivalent to a few candles. I waited for my eyes to adjust further and crept around the room, making for the bed. Hiding behind a massive wardrobe, I paused and listened before glancing at the bed. It was empty. Perhaps he was up using the bathroom?

"You have news?" a deep, gruff voice asked from across the room. There, sitting at a desk with his back to me, was a well-muscled goblin at least fifty percent larger than any we'd seen so far. He was a behemoth, dwarfing me in size and weight. He wore only an undergarment as he studied an open book. A large bastard sword in a leather scabbard rested against the wall halfway between the desk and his bed.

He half-turned his head. "What news, scum?"

I cleared my throat and began to approach. In my best goblin imitation, I said, "Master, all clear. I-I think the teleporter not working."

He paused his writing. "What do mean, teleporter not workin'?" He then turned around. "Hm, visitor."

I dashed forward but he leapt up, grabbing his heavy wooden chair and throwing it with tremendous force. Ducking down, I barely avoided it as it smashed into the wardrobe, shattering to pieces. Before I had recovered, he'd unsheathed his massive sword.

"Been long since faced warrior in combat." He gestured and whispered a command and his lights brightened. He then laughed. "You no warrior. Weak, no-clothes man."

I looked down at my mismatched clothing and small sword. "A warrior is not defined by his equipment." He was making fun of my clothing while he stood there in his underwear.

He nodded. "Dat True. Come, fight."

I moved forward, hoping his charitable demeanor did not change. He could have shouted for his guards. I estimated I had ten minutes before the patrol would be back on an adjoining hall where they could hear him or our battle.

The large goblin took a two-handed stance, with his sword straight up near his right shoulder. "No worry. You my kill. If need guards to kill weakling, then I not fit to be Chief. Long, long time since warriors come here."

He took several steps forward, stepping down from the raised platform the desk sat upon. I moved in the opposite direction, keeping a weight-bearing column and the banister on the back of the platform between us. "There's no need for us to fight. I merely wish to leave."

The goblin warrior chuckled. "We must fight. You must die. Master says no intruders."

"Master? Can I speak to your master?"

"No. Even I no speak to Master, and I Chief. Master busy." He quickened his pace. "Are you warrior or coward? Fight!"

I looked at my sword then back at his. "I hardly think it would be a fair fight."

"You weakling because have tiny sword. Me strong, have big sword."

"Sounds perfectly logical," I said as I started another loop around the room. As I moved, I looked for something that could be used as a weapon.

"Stop running!" the chief roared. He grabbed a bookcase and toppled it over. It crashed into the banister. Sprinting forward, he tried to pen me in, but I leapt upon the back of the case. He had expected me to run away, but instead, I turned and brought my sword down at his neck. He barely raised his sword in time, skidding to a halt before tripping over the case.

I swung several more times, darting in and out. I nicked him twice before he gave up on defense and swung his blade directly at my midsection. I flattened against the bookcase as the blade sliced the air above me. Looking up, I saw the goblin swinging down upon me. He was faster than his size would suggest. Rolling to the side, I barely avoided being split in half. The bookcase wasn't so lucky. The blade cleaved it in two, striking with so much force that the tip plunged into the raised wooden floor.

Hopping up, I grabbed a thick, leather-bound book and slid it down over the sword and grasped it as firmly as I could muster. The goblin jerked the blade free, pulling me along with it. Using the added momentum, I thrust my blade forward, aiming for his throat, but he jerked at the last moment, and I only grazed his shoulder. I let go of his sword just as he brought his large arm up into a backhand which sent me sailing over the bookcase. The impact knocked the breath from me.

The goblin kicked away half of the bookcase and stepped forward, his sword high above his head. "You fight tricky."

"There was no need to fight at all," I said as I kicked upward, planting my foot squarely into his crotch. He doubled over, and I went for this throat again. This time I sliced the side, but he twisted yet again. He grabbed my arm and slung me sideways to get me away while he recovered from my underhanded blow. I smashed through the banister and tumbled across the room. My left arm twisted as I fell on it.

"Too fast for your tricks," the goblin said as he grasped his genitals. He showed me a golden ring on his index finger.

Was he saying the ring had magical properties? That would explain how such a large creature could move so quickly. He was almost as fast as I was despite his bulk.

We recovered as the same time. He kicked his way through the remnants of the railing and approached. Blood oozed down his neck, but he seemed unconcerned. He brought his sword down again, but I swung hard and deflected it, sending it to the side. My whole arm ached and went numb from the force of his strike. I then ran again.

"Stop running!" he screamed. I wasn't sure how much time had passed, but the patrol might have heard that. Zarah would be defenseless unless I could finish the fight quickly. I swapped my sword from my numb right hand to my left, but something was wrong. Although I could grasp the hilt, I couldn't bring my arm up. It was dislocated.

The goblin lunged forward again, swinging wildly. He knew I couldn't defend myself. I moved toward the pillar and leapt back as his swing crashed into the support pillar. A ceiling beam crashed down, along with bits of the ceiling and dust. The chief caught the beam with one arm and kept it from falling farther.

"I too strong!" he bellowed as he struggled to hold up the beam. Through a cloud of dust, my sword appeared, cleaning jabbing directly into his throat. He dropped his massive sword and grasped my blade until blood seeped between his fingers. He pushed it back and me along with it.

"Not die..." he gurgled as blood gushed from the new wound. The chief roared in fury and took a step forward as the beam and bits of the ceiling crashed down around him. When the dust cleared, only one of his hands and a leg were visible under the rubble. Thankfully, the damage was limited to that one area, as the other beams and pillars held, although several creaked ominously. I slipped the ring from the finger of his exposed hand.

Coughing, I exited the room to check on Zarah.

"You've arrived just in time," she said. A torchlight appeared at the end of the hall, accompanied by shouting.

I pulled her into the room and pushed her to the opposite side of the doorway. A moment later, three goblins burst into the room.

They waved away the cloud of dust. "Where Chief?" one asked.

Zarah moved behind the last one and quietly slit his throat but not before he yelped. The other two turned to face her, but I kicked one from behind while stabbing the other in the back. Zarah deftly dodged the off-balance goblin, sending him crashing into the wall. He turned just in time to witness my dagger flying toward his forehead.

Zarah shook her head in false disappointment. "Not very effective warriors, are they?"

I looked at the scrapes, bruises, and my arm and back at her. "Perhaps not these, but their leader was quite capable. I get the feeling they haven't seen combat in recent years."

Zarah spotted the ring in my hand. "A gift?"

I held the ring up to a nearby light. "No. I suspect it will be more useful for me if it is safe." I slipped the ring on my finger, not sure of what to expect. It instantly shrank down to fit, as magical jewelry tended to do.

"What's its enchantment?" Zarah asked. She now seemed to move slightly slower from my perspective.

I waved my hand in front of my face. "It enhances my speed slightly — perhaps my focus and accuracy, too."

She held my hand up and inspected the magical artifact. "It was reckless putting it on without knowing what it does." My arm flopped back down, useless.

"We could have a horde of goblins upon us at any moment. I wanted to be prepared. Since the goblin wore it, I knew it wasn't cursed."

She inspected my shoulder and other injuries. "It's definitely dislocated. Come over here."

I moved to the doorway. "Are you as skilled at medical care as you are with your melodies?"

"Apparently more skilled than you are at avoiding harm. I may have to start charging you," she said as she placed my chest against the wall and grabbed my arm with both of her hands. She braced her leg against the other side. "This may hurt a little." She jerked backward with all her weight and might. I felt something in my shoulder pop.

I looked down at my arm as I flexed it. It was a little numb, and my shoulder hurt, but it functioned again. "Where did you learn that?"

She smiled. "Having spent much of my life in lowlife bars, I've had to treat a variety of wounds." She took a scrap of cloth out and wiped away the blood from several of my cuts.

I moved away from her, searching through the room. "There's no time for that. We need to find the key."

She looked down at the pile of rubble. "I hope it wasn't on him when the ceiling fell."

I moved to the desk and searched through the papers and open books. A large, copper key similar to the previous keys laid near the edge. "No, the key is here." We searched the room and found two other keys which opened the chests at the foot of the chief's bed.

One contained a fair amount of gold and a few small gems. The other contained alcohol. Not watered-down swill like the mead and ale in the barrels we'd found, but pure, distilled alcohol. We stuffed a bottle into our sack along with the gems and gold.

"He's not going to need it anymore, and this is at least twenty years' wages," Zarah said.

I moved to the vanquished goblin guards. They wore leather vests, boots, and gloves. Between the three of them, I assembled a makeshift set of armor, although without leggings. It was loose in some areas — and tight in others — but it was functional. It was a huge relief to finally have protection for my aching feet.

My sword laid buried under the rubble, but one guard carried a stout spear, while the other two wielded longswords. I took the spear and a sword, while Zarah discarded her cleaver in favor of the second sword. I fastened a sword belt above my belt of pouches and sheathed the sword. Zarah did the same and also removed a gray hooded cloak from the smaller goblin.

Feeling better now that I was armed and armored, I returned to the desk. Something had caught my eye while I'd searched for the key. I studied the open book and parchment on the table.

Zarah moved to my side. "What is it?"

"A spellbook. It seems the goblin chief was attempting to teach himself magic. Look here. He was drawing these mystic symbols on the parchment when I entered. He was not a very good artist."

"You're able to read this? You, who don't know your own name?"

I stared at the pages, mouthing the words as I flipped through several of the passages. "I know this language. I can't explain how, but I know many of these words."

"You're messing with dangerous forces if you dabble in sorcery," Zarah warned.

I grabbed the book and placed it in the sack with our food. After a long swig of water, I glanced over the room one more time before motioning for Zarah to join me. "We can't wait to see if the teleporter will reset. With their chief and a patrol killed, they will begin to search the floor for intruders. We'll have to take our chances on the next floor."

She nodded and we quickly crept down the hall. Without a patrol to worry about, we could move faster. Soon, we found another metal door that was identical to the ones that connected the floors. I wondered if there was any significance to the fact that these doors were designed differently from the others.

Zarah ignited a torch and held it into the open doorway, illuminating the steps down. "Are you sure we should do this? There might be something worse than goblins down there."

I thought about it. We were bettered armed now, but a horde of angry goblins would prove too much for the pair of us. Sword readied, I took the first step down.

"We'll have to risk it."

CHAPTER ELEVEN
Unexpected

At the base of the stairwell, we found evidence of the supplies the goblins had left. Bits of food, crumbs, and other tidbits covered the floor in the small room before the metal door.

"Something intelligent lives on this floor," I remarked.

Zarah looked through the small, barred window. "We lie in wait and ambush them."

"No, I don't want to fight in this confined space. We need to explore the area."

Zarah yawned. "I'm exhausted, and you need medical attention and rest. Perhaps we could sleep, soon?

She was right. The battle with the goblin chief had left me fatigued, and we'd both been up all night. "We'll see if we can find a fortified room we can rest in."

I gently opened the door, closed it behind us, and locked it.

"What if they have another key?" Zarah asked.

Taking a bit of the rope, I cut off a portion and stuffed the lock full of it, leaving part of it hanging from our side. "I don't want to completely block our escape, but this should delay them if they try and follow us. They don't seem that intelligent."

Carefully, we made our way down the new passage. Silence hung heavy in the air. Upon entering the floor above, the sense that something lived and breathed could be felt immediately, but this floor felt...dead. In fact, the cloying odor of decay lingered.

The first room we found had no door and was completely empty. We continued until we found a bedroom with a stout, heavy door. I barred the door from the inside and moved a dusty dresser in front of it. It slid easily across the floor. On a whim, I lifted it several inches off the floor.

Zarah noticed my feat of strength. "Trying to show off?"

"I'm surprised at how light this is, that's all," I replied as I set it down.

She moved to piece of furniture, squatted, and tried to move it. She looked at me with surprise. "No, this is heavy, dense wood."

"I suppose food, rest, and battle have reinvigorated my sinews," I said as I looked down at my arms. Thick veins strained against my skin.

"Perhaps..." Zarah replied.

The bed had decayed to the point where it had collapsed. Zarah cleared off an area on the floor for our makeshift bedding and blankets. She found a candle and lit it, dousing her torch. She then unpacked a few bits of food.

I flopped down and devoured the food quickly. I hadn't realized how hungry I'd grown. Adrenaline and fear had fueled me for the last few hours. My eyes grew heavy as my exertions caught up with me.

After eating, I removed my armor and set it in the corner of the room. Zarah inspected my fresh wounds before she began cleaning them. "Nothing too serious. You're either extremely lucky, or a fairly skilled fighter. You still don't recall anything of your past? Were you a soldier? A guard? You're too muscular for an average villager, unless you were perhaps a blacksmith or stone mason."

"No. It's beyond frustrating. I know many things — apparently even ancient magic languages, but not my own name."

She dabbed her cloth in a bit of the pure alcohol. I grimaced as she rubbed it on a deep cut. It felt like she'd poured liquid fire on the wound. "Knowing how to defend yourself at the moment is a more useful skill than knowing your name. Still, I should have something to call you."

"You think of something. I'm beyond the capacity for thought at the moment," I said as I lay face down on the floor.

She once again began to massage my tender muscles. It felt as if more of my body was bruised than wasn't. "Kain? Varn?"

"It's up to you. I have no preference."

She paused and offered, "Hero?"

I chuckled. "Hero? That's a profession, not a name."

"I feel it would do you a disservice to give you a name that is not your true name. But you are a hero."

I turned over and looked up at her. "No, a hero is one that sacrifices his or her welfare for others. I'm merely a confused man trying to survive an unusual situation."

"No, you risked yourself for me, which makes you a hero."

"I helped someone in need, which merely makes me a human."

Zarah laughed. "I've met thousands of so-called 'humans' while working in various bars. Believe me, someone who would risk their own life for others is a rarity. You must have a code of honor or justice if you're willing to do that."

She lay down beside me, pulled up the makeshift blanket, and turned sideways to face me.

"If I do, I don't recall it. I suppose I just couldn't let someone suffer under the power of someone as cruel as that beast man."

"And I supposed my being a beautiful woman had nothing to do with it?"

I thought about it for a moment. "No. It had nothing at all to do with it. I would have done the same for anyone who was suffering."

"What if I deserved it? What if I'd murdered someone? Shouldn't I be punished?"

I wasn't sure of the purpose of her theoretical line of questioning, but I could barely remain awake. "Those that are guilty should be punished. If you are guilty of something, then perhaps fate will punish you at a later time. I am too tired to continue this conversation."

Zarah posed one more question. "Aren't we all guilty of something?"

I yawned and turned over. "If I am, I am ignorant of it at the moment. Thank you for tending my wounds. Good night."

I AWOKE AT SOME POINT to find Zarah's arm draped across me. The room felt a bit colder than when we'd entered, which was unusual. I'd noticed that the temperatures within the structure seemed to remain fairly static, which made sense as we were descending farther underground.

I removed her arm and relieved myself in the far corner. As silly as it seemed, I felt slightly embarrassed to do so in her presence, and I also felt guilt at using the restroom indoors, but this room contained no chamber pot like some of the others. We were already overladen with weapons, armor, and supplies, and carting around a fetid chamber pot would be impossible.

I fumbled in the darkness and returned to our makeshift bed. I stared into the pitch-black abyss and listened. Crushing fear descended upon my mind as I imagined the horrors I'd witnessed on the floors above. What awaited us? It felt as if we were moving away from salvation, not toward it. We were alone inside a godforsaken nightmare. Zarah's soft breathing reassured me. I wasn't alone.

She was not a disciplined warrior, but her presence provided a type of armor to my sanity. I thought of her songs and of her gentle touch. My mind involuntarily turned to her beautiful face, and then her supple nude form stretched out and bound on the rack, where I'd found her. I turned over and tried to think of something else. The only memories I could access at the moment were of my captivity within this heinous place. Again, my mind turned to Zarah as I drifted off to sleep. She reminded me of...someone. My mind refused to tell me who.

"HERO, THERE'S SOMETHING outside."

I blinked at the darkness, trying to force myself to focus. My sleep-deprived brain was still groggy. A faint shuffle sounded from the hall. It faded within a second.

"I was afraid it would try and get in," Zarah whispered in my ear.

I lit a candle and listened again. "Whatever it was, it seems to be gone."

We dressed and packed our things, eating a light breakfast. It was impossible to tell the time of day. It could be the middle of the night or late in the morning, but we had no way of knowing. We'd just have to judge the time by our bodies' signals.

While Zarah finished packing the bedding, I studied the spellbook. As a beginner-level book, it did not contain any devastating spells of great power, but it did have useful spells. Ones for opening simple locks, providing light, and...detecting magic. I looked at the ring on my finger and studied the spell intently.

I set the book and candle on top of the dresser, pulled out my knife and began carving symbols on the top of the dresser. I then set the ring in the center of the arcane characters and attempted to decipher the words of the spell. An experienced magic user could forgo using the focusing symbols, but I would need them. "De-Desi...Desicry"

Zarah looked up from her packing. "You're going to blow us up or turn me into a toad."

"Not with this spell," I said as I continued to enunciate the words. "Desicry Arcenarum."

The ring began to glow. I looked over at my shoulder at Zarah, smiling mischievously.

She frowned. "We already knew it was magical."

"Yes, which makes it the perfect object to test this spell on. If we did not know it was magical, I'd have no way to determine if I was merely reading the spell wrong or if the object lacked any magical properties. This means I do have the capacity to learn and use magic."

Something on the wall behind her caught my attention. Glowing symbols faded into view, obviously magical in origin. "There's something scrawled on the wall." The symbols resembled a few I'd seen in the spellbook.

I flipped through the pages and compared them to similar images. "They look like partial summoning glyphs, but I believe they are incomplete."

Zarah traced her finger around one. "Why do they react to your spell if they aren't complete?"

I flipped through the book but found no answer. According to what I'd learned so far, they should be inert. "I don't know." I stared at the glowing ring and turned to another spell.

After several attempts at pronunciation, I said, "Illusterate Visnera Decalarum!"

Above the ring, glowing words in a white-blue glowing font appeared. It was an older version of Common, so easily read. "Ring of Speed, I. Crafter: Woll Yaoghun."

"I've never seen that before," Zarah said as she leaned over my shoulder.

"It's a minor identification spell. It's common for practitioners of the magical arts to sign the artifacts they create. Usually they include the purpose of the object and the crafter's name. It works as a form of advertisement, as well as a matter of pride."

Zarah nodded. "Why not just engrave it into the material?"

"Have you seen the prices engravers charge? This is inexpensive and it would of course be difficult to engrave an amulet or ring with all of that information."

Zarah turned to face me. "Perhaps I should call you Sorcerer instead of Hero. You know more about magic than any common man I've met."

"Yes, perhaps I am an apprentice to a magic user, but don't recall."

"Or you could be a librarian. Although I've never seen a librarian or magic apprentice fight as you do."

I slipped the ring onto my finger and gave the room one last look. "I'd rather find out once we're free. Regardless of what I was before I lost my memory, what I am now is a man trapped in this...dungeon or whatever it may be."

"There are old songs about places like this. Ancient places of power, where the dead live again and monsters roam. Filled with treasure and danger. Many of the songs are quite romantic."

I cracked open the door and listened for a moment before answering. "Those tall tales were created to inspire dreamers and frighten children." I lit a torch and stepped into the hall.

Zarah followed me out of the room. "Yet, this place fits the descriptions from legend perfectly."

We advanced through the hall, inspecting each room as we went. This floor seemed to be made up of living quarters, but the layout gave the suggestion that there was a massive room somewhere.

"This floor seems to be uninhabited," Zarah whispered as we proceeded.

"The goblins were leaving food for some—" I began to say before the stone under my foot sank into the ground. "Get back!" I shouted as I grabbed Zarah and jumped backward.

Three metal spikes descended from the ceiling and stopped short with a nerve-rattling screech. We dusted ourselves off and gathered our dropped items. Curious, I tapped the spikes with the butt of my spear. They did not move.

I ducked under the spikes. "Careful — the mechanism is rusted, but it could break free."

Zarah quickly moved beneath the trap. "As if the denizens of this place were not enough trouble, someone has laid traps for us."

"Not for us. This trap is perhaps two or three hundred years old. Look at the amount of rust. We'll have to be more careful; the next one may not be faulty."

Zarah nodded. "You keep an eye out for creatures, and I'll try and focus on the stonework and other anomalies. I've got very good eyesight."

"Agreed. This place becomes deadlier the deeper we travel."

The air hung heavy with the scent of decay and filth, but I was unable to locate the source. It set my nerves on edge, as if walking through a graveyard. I chuckled mentally — I had no memory of ever traversing a graveyard, yet I was comparing my current situation to it. I assumed that meant I must have done so at some point in my life. It was like my ability to decipher the language of the spellbook, yet I couldn't remember my family, my name, or any life experiences. It was unnerving.

We encountered another trap not long after. A tripwire from one side of the wall to another. The impossibly thin strand escaped my notice, but Zarah's keen eyesight caught it a moment before my foot tripped it. My first instinct was to trigger it with my spear, but there was no telling what the result would be. We stepped over it. I marked both sides of the wall with our torch, scorching the stone as a marker.

We arrived back at the door that led back up to the previous floor. I checked my sabotage on the lock and found it undisturbed.

Zarah sighed in frustration. "Are we trapped?"

"No. I wanted to explore the outer perimeter of this floor before we took one of the side passages that led inward. I was hoping we'd find an unlocked door down, but perhaps there is another teleporter or stairwell in the center of this floor. Using this method, we won't be surprised and driven toward the middle, because the only threats can come from the center."

Zarah shrugged. "Unless there are invisible doors and secret passages."

"Yes, but I'd exhaust myself by using the detect magic spell every ten feet in order to locate any magic doors. It taxes my stamina to cast even those low-level spells. Just as an athlete must build up his endurance for sporting events, a spellcaster must build up his magical endurance to cast spells. We'll have to risk it."

"I guess we'd better just hope nothing's going to pop out once we've got our backs turned, eh?" Zarah said as she started walking down a hall that they had yet to explore.

Only a few storage rooms and closets lined this hall. I noticed something curious. "Does it feel like this passage is at a decline to you? I feel as if it's running downhill slightly."

Zarah looked at the floor and thought about it. "Yes, I believe you're right."

Ahead, two other passages combined at a massive door. It was composed of a dark, red wood with ornate scenes of hapless victims being tortured in obscene and disturbing ways. We took a moment to study the carvings. At the top of the door, a phrase was etched in an old style of font. I read it aloud in case Zarah was unfamiliar with the language. "Through Pain, There Is Justice." Underneath that phrase was a symbol of a man with his arms crossed in front of him. Barbed vines encircled his body.

Zarah traced her finger around the figure of a man being split in half by a saw. "I'm not sure I want to enter this place." She inspected her finger. Was she was testing for dust or blood?

I checked my equipment and weapons and tightened the straps on my armor. "We have to forge ahead. The only other way out is up — unless there are secret doors — but we could spend days searching before we might stumble upon one."

Zarah looked worried. "Do you think it's another torture chamber?"

"We shall see," I said as I shoved the double doors. They swung inward with more force than I'd expected. Blinding light caused us to shield our eyes. It was if a red sun had been born before us.

Scarcely able to believe the scene before me, I finally whispered, "It's a...church."

CHAPTER TWELVE
Buried Faith

The huge room looked as if could house several hundred people. Row after row of pews were immaculately arranged in perfect alignment. Their polished dark wood shone in the dazzling light emitted from the windows. Red velvety carpet lined the aisles. Images of torture similar to the ones engraved in the door were frozen in the stained-glass windows, which were made up of shards of deep reds, yellows, and greens. Massive golden chandeliers dangled on thick chains hung from the high ceilings.

At the far end of the room, a gargantuan stage contained a single pulpit that looked to be carved from a sturdy stone. Long, thick drapes lined the back of the stage.

"What-what is this place?" Zarah asked as the light from the room illuminated her bright blue eyes with reddish rays that made them appear purple.

I pointed down to the front row of pews. "Perhaps she can tell us."

A lone figure sat silently as if praying. We glanced around the room and down the hall before we made our way down the aisle.

"This carpet is heavenly," Zarah said with a blissful look on her face. I'd forgotten she wore no shoes.

"Hail!" I shouted down. There was no response. Zarah and I looked at each other.

"Perhaps it's a trap?"

I gripped my sword tighter. "There's only one way to find out." I walked the remaining distance down and observed the woman. No, it was a girl. Perhaps thirteen, with dowdy brown hair that looked as if she'd cut it herself. She wore a clean but basic hooded black and red robe and cloth slippers. Her pale skin took a reddish hue in the room's illumination. Hands clasped, her head was bowed in prayer.

"Can you hear me?" I asked.

She continued praying. We listened to her prayers but were unable to make out the words from her low muttering.

Zarah cocked her head to the side. "Perhaps she's deaf and blind? Many of the daft and infirm are sent to nunneries."

The girl finished her prayer and opened her dark brown eyes. "No, I can hear you perfectly fine. It's rude to interrupt someone's prayer. Have you no manners?"

Zarah looked at me in astonishment for bursting out in laughter. "You're right, young miss. Accept my humble apologies. My name is Zarah Telon. This is my...companion, er...Hero."

The girl looked at me with suspicion. "Hero is an odd name. What's your real name?"

"I'm afraid I've lost my memory. Hero is what she has taken to calling me."

She looked as if she wasn't sure what she thought about this strange situation before finally saying, "I'm Emlee."

I nodded. "It's nice to meet you, Emlee. Now, if you don't mind, I'd like to know just what you're doing in here?"

"I'm praying."

"Why?" Zarah asked.

"Because the goblins told me to when I first came here. They locked me down here and told me I must pray every day or bad things would happen."

"How long have you been here?" I asked.

"I...don't know. A long time. Did the goblins bring you here to pray with me?"

I looked around the room. "No, we are trying to escape from this place. Do you know of an exit? How is there sunlight coming through these windows when we are deep in the earth? Have you tried to break them?"

"No. There is no way to escape. The goblins said so," Emlee answered.

I approached one of the stained-glass windows and touched the tip with my sword. It sounded liked glass. Pushing harder, I waited for it to crack, but it held fast. I reared back my arm and slammed the blade into the beautiful pane, eliciting a rain of sparks.

"Desicry Arcenarum." A faint blue glow radiated from the edges of the false windows. They were some type of solid illusions. Nothing but the stone walls waited behind them. A false hope, dashed again.

Emlee frowned. "I told you there was no way out."

I motioned for Zarah to join me and walked a short distance away from the girl. "What do you think?"

Zarah glanced over her shoulder at Emlee, but kept her voice low. "I'm not sure. Why kidnap a girl and force her to pray?"

"Perhaps she is keeping some ancient evil at bay? I wonder if this is the bottom of the dungeon. If she has been here as long as she's said, surely she could have found an exit by now. Something doesn't feel right."

I approached Emlee. "Was there anyone else with you when they brought you here? How have you managed to survive so long?"

"No, it was just me. The goblins give me food and water every few days...unless they forget. Then I bang on the door until they remember me."

"That's awful," Zarah said.

"Have you come to rescue me and take me back to my family?"

I looked at Zarah then back at Emlee. "We will take you home. Just give us some time to come up with a plan. Where do you stay?"

"I sleep in the little storage room behind the stage. The goblins gave me some bedding and blankets, although I had to carry them myself."

"It seems the goblins don't want to come down here for some reason," I said.

"Perhaps they're afraid of whatever she's praying against?" Zarah said.

"Emlee, what are you praying for? Are you praying to a certain god, like Pilon?"

"I'm praying to Castigous," she said.

"Castigous?" I gasped. No one prayed to Castigous in the modern era. He was a relic of the past. As the god of punishment and vengeance, older civilizations prayed for him to punish their enemies.

The carvings and stained-glass artwork now made sense. Pain and misery were all Castigous had to offer humanity. Was this entire structure devoted to him? I thought of the torture chamber above and its horrendous devices, as well as the cells throughout dungeon.

Emlee showed me a faded scrap of paper. It was a page from the Aeon Torment — the bible of Castigous' followers.

"The wicked and false will split and steam. The unjust will rot and scream. Death has no power here, your suffering will..." I whispered as I read the page. It was some sort of twisted psalm, followed by a short prayer.

"O' Castigous, flay my body and soul and drive the wickedness from me. Destroy my sin and reshape my thoughts. Mold me to your will so that I may serve you and righteous justice. Amen."

Zarah knelt in front of Emlee and took the young girl's hands in hers. "You poor thing. Forced to pray to a god of evil and alienated from anyone else for all this time."

Emlee stared at Zarah for a long moment as if analyzing her. An awkward silence followed. Zarah stepped away and pulled her cloak over her head. "It gives me the chills just thinking about it. This is a temple of evil." Emlee continued to watch Zarah. Was the young girl ensorcelled? Perhaps her weeks or months of prayer had brainwashed her, and Zarah had offended her. Her isolation could have affected her mind. Even an adult would suffer under such conditions.

"We will escape and take you with us. Does that sound good?" I asked.

Emlee broke her gaze from Zarah. "How? We'll die if we try and escape. Castigous will punish us."

"Did the goblins tell you that? It's a lie. If there is no way out on this floor, we will fight our way back through the floor above." I wasn't sure if that was wise, but I needed to convince Emlee that escape was possible. A hysterical young girl could draw attention or distract us from noticing a trap.

"Have you explored this floor? You've found no secret doors or clues as to a way out?" I asked Emlee.

Emlee shook her head. "There is no way out. I've looked everywhere. Every day I searched."

"Do you know what is causing the smell? We found no bodies, but the smell of death permeates this entire floor," I asked.

"Except in here," Zarah said.

I sniffed the air. This room smelled old and musty, but the scent of decay was missing. Curious.

"No, it only smells bad outside. My prayers keep this room purified," Emlee said.

Zarah looked around the room. "I guess we'll be spending the night in here, then. This carpet will be a pleasure to sleep on, in comparison to the stone floor."

"No! You can't stay in here. You are not a believer. You aren't even supposed to be in here!" Emlee shouted. The change in her demeanor was unsettling.

"It will be okay; nothing is going to —" I began.

"No! It's forbidden! You have to stay outside!" the girl screamed. She was becoming hysterical.

"Now, look — if you think we're going to —" Zarah said, but Emlee started to push her out.

"You must go! I must begin my prayers again!"

I grabbed the young girl's arm. "Who did this to you?" Her arms were covered in remarkable tattoos. She jerked her arm from my grasp and covered her arms with the sleeves of her robe.

"The...goblins did that."

The topic struck a nerve with her. I could tell she was ashamed of them. Once again, she moved to usher us from the room.

Zarah looked as if she was about to restrain the girl, but I put my hand on her shoulder. "We will go. This is her sanctuary. We need to respect her wishes."

"I don't see why we need to sleep out in that rot-smelling room on the floor when there is a perfectly fine —" Zarah said.

"It's fine. Another night on the stone floor will not harm us. We've both endured worse," I said as I led Zarah back toward the large door. I turned around and noticed Emlee had resumed her prayers.

In the hall outside, Zarah pulled me aside. "Why are we allowing a child to dictate where we sleep?"

I led her away from the church, back toward the room we'd occupied last night. "Because I believe there is more to this situation than we've seen."

Zarah waited for me to continue before finally asking, "Are you going to explain your suspicions?"

"No, I'd prefer to hold them for now. I know it's frustrating, but trust me."

We set up our camp again, and I barricaded the door. Once inside, I began to study the spellbook while Zarah prepared our lunch.

She took a bite of an apple and said, "If we're going to be here long, we'll need more supplies. Over half our water is gone already. We could drink the alcohol, I suppose."

I shook my head. "No, alcohol will dehydrate us. We'll need to obtain water. Perhaps Emlee will have some we can share."

"Do you have a plan for escape? I'm sure the goblins have discovered their chief is dead by now. They'll probably be furious and looking for us. If there really is no way down from this floor, then we're trapped."

I glanced up from the book. "I find it odd the goblins refuse to set foot on this floor and leave the supplies for Emlee in the stairwell. There's something they fear down here."

"I have felt uneasy since we've arrived here. The smell of death, the feeling that there is something just out of sight that's watching us. Do you think it has something to do with these symbols on the walls?"

"Perhaps. This symbol is incomplete, so it shouldn't work. This book teaches the basics of summoning, but a symbol like that is much more advanced than the lessons available in this spellbook. I'm quickly learning some of the more basic spells, however."

"Like what? Maybe a way to teleport us out of here?"

"Illuminous Manifestae," I whispered, gesturing into the air above the desk. A small, bright blue orb blazed into existence.

It was slightly dimmer than a torch, but quite a bit brighter than the candle I'd been using to study.

Zarah stood and approached the magical sphere. She tentatively reached out to the floating light.

I smiled. "It's safe. It has no physical form and does not generate heat."

She attempted to touch it, but her hand passed through. "I've seen a sorcerer's apprentice use it in a show once. Does this mean we can stop carrying these dirty torches around?"

"No. With my current energy reserves, I could only cast one that should last a few hours. We'll still need the torches and candles for now. It's possible to cast one that lasts days, weeks, or even months. The glowing orbs in the dungeon are probably based on a similar spell, but I don't know from where they'd draw their power."

Zarah nodded in approval before trying to entrap the sphere in part of our bedding. "It's strange. It's here, and yet it isn't."

I cupped my hands around the orb. Rays of lights slipped between my fingers. I then let my hands pass through it. "It does have curious properties." I returned to the book and continued my studies. Zarah began humming a tune. I relaxed and felt my mind become more focused. I wondered if her melody was enhancing me in some way or if it merely made me feel at ease, able to focus despite our predicament. I thought to ask her, but an interesting paragraph pulled my attention back to the spellbook.

My orb of light began to sputter. "What?" I said. "It's too soon for the spell to expire."

"You've been reading for hours," Zarah said, stretching. "I dozed off at some point. There isn't much to do."

I felt a slight pang of guilt at leaving her to fend for herself. The spellbook had held my attention completely. It had felt like I'd started reading minutes ago, but time had advanced rapidly. "It must be dusk or later," I guessed.

Zarah handed me an orange. "Who can say? This darkness is maddening. Perhaps it's morning or midnight."

I hadn't noticed how hungry I'd become. I split open the orange and ate a quarter of it in one bite. The fruits and vegetables we'd taken from the kitchen staved off hunger, but I'd grown tired of such light fair. Thoughts of the pig-man's stew came into my mind unbidden, and I found myself salivating involuntarily.

After slaking my thirst from the waterskin, a weariness came over me. I stood from the desk and almost fell.

"What's wrong?" Zarah said as she rushed to my side.

"I've just suddenly become tired. Exhausted, in fact."

Zarah helped me to the bed. "We haven't done anything all day except walk around. Perhaps you need more food?"

"It could be that, but more likely it's the casting I've been doing. I perhaps overextended myself. A good night's rest will replenish my reserves."

She tucked me in and checked a few of her makeshift bandages. "At least tonight there are no new wounds or bruises."

Her gentle caresses and attention eased my mind. I drifted off into uneasy slumber.

CHAPTER THIRTEEN
Unearthed

"Hero, wake up."

Zarah whispered in my ear while holding her hand over my mouth. "Something's outside."

Lying still, I held my breath and listened. Something was shuffling down the hall. No, there were several sets of footsteps. I mentally cursed myself for being so lax on security. I quietly slipped out from under the blanket. I donned my clothes and armor. Fortunately, Zarah's assistance sped up the process tremendously.

She dressed and grabbed her sword. Our gear was packed already, except for the bedding, which she quickly rolled up. In her haste, her sword tip clanked against the stone floor. "Sorry," she whispered.

Perhaps whatever wandered the halls hadn't heard. We listened for minutes, but the shuffling had ceased.

My eyes were heavy from lack of sleep. It felt like three or four in the morning.

Zarah lit a candle. She looked as tired as I felt. "We searched the floor. There's no one else here."

"There could be any number of passages we failed to discover."

"What about Emlee? Will she be safe?"

"She's been safe this long, so I expect so. We'll have to ask her if she knows anything in the morning," I said.

I sat on the floor and motioned for Zarah to sit. "I'll take first watch; if I see anything, I'll —"

Zarah's eyes grew wide with fright as she pointed toward the door. The top of the door bent inward as if something was pushing against it. The dresser tilted slightly from the pressure.

I leapt to my feet and moved to the side of the door. I motioned for her to take up a position to my left and to cover her eyes.

The door creaked as the force on the other side increased. A low moan escaped from the lips of the intruder. The frame of the door cracked, and the door swept inward.

"Illuminous Manifestae!" I shouted as I averted my gaze. The blindingly bright orb flared to life in front of the intruder. It groaned in protest and shielded its eyes. I stabbed it in the torso with my sword. It easily slid into the flesh of our foe — too easily. A wave of stench filled the room as the intruder pushed its way into our room.

It grabbed my wrist and held it fast. I was confused by its lack of reaction from being stabbed. Wresting my arm from its grasp, I stumbled back. My eyes having now adjusted, I could now see why the creature had not reacted to my sword thrust.

A grotesque undead man stumbled toward us. His clothes and flesh had rotted together until one could not be discerned from the other. Decayed skin sloughed from his bones with each wobbling step he took. While the flesh and muscle around his face was mostly intact, the bright white bone of his frontal skull gleamed in the dim light. A single eye swiveled between Zarah and me as if attempting to identify the greater threat.

I swung my sword again. The creature attempted to block the blade with its hand but only ended up losing its fingers. Zarah gagged as the severed digits bounced off of the wall.

The creature reached out with its other hand, but Zarah dashed around the side and hacked at its leg. It turned to face her. It seemed to feel no pain from our attacks, which made fighting it difficult. I used the opportunity to swing at its neck. My blade bit deep and severed most of the connective tissue. The decaying head flopped to the side, now peering at us upside down. After a moment of confusion, it resumed its attack on Zarah.

I slashed at its neck again, severing the last bit of flesh attaching the head to the body. The body collapsed and remained immobile.

Zarah looked as if she were about to vomit but resisted. "What manner of creature was that?"

I wiped the creature's disgusting fluids from my sword onto the edge of the dresser. "A ghoul. My memory is fuzzy, but apparently the reanimation magic that gives them sentience and mobility is tied to their heads."

Zarah gathered our belongings. "Where did it come from?"

"We will find out," I said as I lit a torch and peered into the hallway. The smell was almost a physical assault on our senses.

"There are more here. Listen," I said as I raised the torch high. Combined with the orb of light, our visibility was increased about twenty percent. The sound of feet shuffling down the hall came from ahead.

Zarah turned to move the other way but halted and gasped. "They're here, too!"

"Press forward!" I said as I sheathed my sword and grasped my spear firmly. I handed Zarah the torch. The blue orb of light followed us as we moved ahead.

Two ghouls stumbled into our view. Without hesitating, I jabbed the spear through the head of the first one and whipped it free before the second one could react. My next thrust erupted from the rear of his skull. I leaned into each attack, putting my full strength and body weight into it. If I missed or failed to sever their link to their bodies, they'd grab the spear and I'd have to engage in close combat. Another ghoul stumbled into view.

"They are gaining on us from behind!" Zarah shouted. I stabbed the third ghoul, but he raised his hand before the blow landed. The tip passed through his hand and stopped short. He then grabbed the shaft with his other hand. Lunging forward, I ripped my sword from its sheath and removed his head in one blow. The power of my strikes surprised me. Stomping on the creature's hand, I pulled the spear free. My heart thundered from the physical exertion. Rivulets of sweat poured down my brow, stinging my eyes. We were going to be overwhelmed at this rate.

Zarah began to hum a tune. My heart rate slowed. A calmness settled over me. Another ghoul stepped into view only to be dispatched immediately. Another stepped in to take its place.

"We need to make for the church," I said as I sliced at the new ghoul.

Zarah paused her melody. "The doors don't lock. We'll be trapped inside."

"The doors are thick and stout. The pews are in good condition. Even if I can't build a solid barricade, it will give us one direction to defend instead of two," I said as I kicked the ghoul into a wall, then jabbed my spear through its eye socket.

"Have a care. My song of endurance has a limit. It'll lose its effectiveness in a few minutes. You'll start to grow weary again very quickly," she said before she began humming again.

"I'll just have to fight harder," I said as I stepped over the bodies of the destroyed ghouls. Slime, brain matter, and other putrid juices puddled around the bodies. I hoped they possessed no malignant properties — Zarah's feet were still unprotected. I wished I could remember more about the creatures.

Zarah deftly danced across the floor, somehow managing to avoid the various substances. Apparently, singing wasn't her only talent.

The hall leading to the church came into view. Three ghouls stood between us and our goal.

"Where do they keep coming from?" Zarah asked as she watched the hall behind us.

I pointed to the disturbed stones in the walls and floors ahead of us. "They are buried all around us." Almost on cue, a hand erupted from the wall and grabbed my spear just as I'd thrust it at an approaching ghoul. The interference spoiled my aim, causing the tip to pierce its chest. It then grabbed the shaft with both hands. Another arm emerged from the wall, grabbing hold of my weapon. Despite their deteriorated state, whatever animated the creatures provided them with almost superhuman strength. They ripped the spear free from my grasp, breaking it in half in the process.

"I've lost the spear," I shouted over my shoulder. Another hand pushed through the stones in the floor. I leapt over it and kicked the ghoul holding the broken spear. It fell to the floor but did not release it. Spinning around, I decapitated the one behind it before shoving the third one back with an elbow to its face. It toppled back but began to rise again immediately.

I motioned for Zarah to join me down the hall leading to the church. "Hurry!" Despite her humming, I could feel my heart racing again. The hall to the church contained no enemies. We rushed in and slammed the heavy doors closed behind us. Together, we moved many of the rear pews in front of the doors. I set several in front of the doors sideways, then placed several against those as braces. By the time we were done, half a ton of wood now rested against the doors. Collapsing to my knees, I tried to catch my breath.

Zarah sat beside me and looked over her shoulder at the door. "Will it hold?"

"If...the ones remaining...are as strong...as the ones we faced...I...believe so."

"What are you doing here?" Emlee asked from the stage.

Zarah stood. "Are you deaf? Don't you hear those groans and bashing on the other side of the doors?"

Emlee looked past us. "What...have you done?"

"Child, we haven't done a damn thing. These undead creatures just came up from the floors and walls. How could you have not seen them before?" Zarah asked.

"You've offended Castigous! This is his punishment!" Emlee shouted. Her face contorted in anger. "You've ruined everything!"

She stepped down from the stage and kneeled.

"It's too late for prayers. We need to find a way out of here," Zarah said. The doors bowed inward slightly. It sounded like at least five or six ghouls now raged on the other side of the barrier.

I lay down on one of the remaining pews and stared up at the ceiling. Dozens of massive wooden beams branched off from one center point. Wooden planks covered the earthen ceiling. From the inside, a worshiper would not have known this church was buried deep below the earth.

Zarah looked back toward the barricade. "It sounds like their numbers are growing."

I closed my eyes. "I imagine eventually there will be enough to fill up this entire structure."

"How would you know that?"

"Did you notice their decayed garb? Their robes are identical to the one Emlee wears."

Zarah's voice became strained. "There would be hundreds, then. We have no hope of overcoming that number. We're as good as dead."

"As long as we live, there is hope. Fear leads to panic. Panic leads to mistakes. We must rest and think. They have numbers, but we are more intelligent than all of them combined."

"Sometimes there's just no way out of a situation."

"Yes, but we have not arrived at that point yet," I said as I exhaled. I let my mind wander through the events that had transpired thus far. There had to be a way to escape. Emlee was the key.

Hours passed. Zarah paced the center aisle, becoming more agitated as the moans and hammering fists grew louder. "Have you thought of something?"

I stood and approached Emlee. "You are positive there are no other doors or ways out of this room?"

She ignored me and continued to pray.

"She's not going to be any help. We'll have to fight them off somehow," Zarah said as she eyed the door.

I reached down and jerked Emlee to her feet. She looked at me in surprise before grappling with me. "Let me go!" she shrieked as she flailed about.

"We need to know if you know anything. About the ghouls or a way out. Stop kneeling and help us, girl!" I shouted.

Grabbing her more firmly, I dragged her to the far end of the room. "You hear that? It sounds like there are around two hundred of them out there now. Their numbers are growing. You know something about this, don't you? Tell us!"

"Leave me be!" she said as she scratched the side of my face. My anger flared and I backhanded her. She fell to the ground.

"Hero!" Zarah said as she rushed to the young girl's side.

The pews began to slide across the thick carpet as the doors slowly opened. Bracing myself against one, I attempted to halt their progress but was pushed back. The crowd of undead men and women spilled into the room like a slow-moving mudslide.

Zarah helped Emlee to her feet and began humming again. I slashed at the foremost ghoul, cutting its throat but missing the muscle, tendons, and spine. Several closed in from the sides, forcing me back.

Zarah backed away, guiding Emlee. "What do we do?"

We huddled together as the undead creatures moved throughout the room. Instead of coming at us in a single file, which may have given is a slim chance, they were going to surround us.

"Emlee, tell us what you know about these horrors!" I shouted over my shoulder.

We backed up until we were forced to climb onto the stage. The ghouls moved to both ends of the platform, crawling and stepping over each other as they climbed the few steps. The entire church was almost filled with them now. Like a sermon from a devil.

I looked back at Emlee and Zarah. Zarah glanced around the room, her eyes filled with fright. She held Emlee in a protective hug with one arm while waving her sword about with her other. It looked as if she had given up hope.

"Desicry Arcenarum!" I shouted.

"How is that going to help —" Zarah began to ask before I dashed at her with my sword.

My sword pierced Emlee's heart and exited her back. She looked at me in confusion and pain before coughing up a frothy mixture of blood and saliva.

"Why?" Emlee whispered as strength faded from her body.

Zarah looked at me with a mixture of fear and anger. "Are you mad?" she said as she lowered the young girl to the ground.

"Look around," I said as I motioned toward the approaching ghouls.

Zarah's mouth fell open. "They've stopped."

The crowd of undead swayed in place as if awaiting instruction.

"How...did you know?" Emlee asked as blood pooled around her.

I leaned down and examined her arms. The patterns embedded in her flesh still glowed. "There were several clues. First, you stated you've explored this entire floor many times, yet none of the traps had been set off — until we arrived. Secondly, you said the sigils on your arms were drawn by the goblins above, yet their chief can barely craft simple magical designs, much less the intricate ones that adorn your arms. Thirdly, the symbols on your arms illuminated as a result of my detect magic spell. I noticed during our struggle that they appear to be the missing portions of the diagrams that are hidden throughout the rest of the floor, like the one in our room. This entire floor is a mass summoning circle made of smaller circles. Once you activate the symbols on your arms, the circles complete and these undead are summoned. Correct?"

Emlee struggled to breathe, then smiled. Her teeth were covered in blood. When she spoke, her voice was filled with hate and belonged to a woman decades older than the girl before us. "You're smarter than many others who made it this far. They joined my congregation. This girl's body would have served me for many years, but you've ruined it!" She lashed out with talon-like fingernails, but I caught her wrist.

A coughing fit followed, then her death spasms. She fell quiet before a cold wind blew through the room. The ghouls collapsed simultaneously. We backed away from Emlee's body as a transparent image of a haggard woman began to pull herself out of it, much like a person emerging from a well. Her shaggy black hair and torn clothes indicated a wraith born from torment.

"You are fortunate that I am...weak...at the moment. You...don't possess a weapon capable of harming me," she hissed. She struggled to approach us, but then fell back as if she'd fainted. She hovered in the air a moment before beginning to sink. The incorporeal figure gently passed through the stage and out of sight.

Zarah felt for Emlee's pulse. "She's dead."

"Her soul was displaced by that apparition. She hasn't been truly alive for a while. We merely cleansed her body of an intruder. If that spirit had left of her own volition, this girl would be nothing but an empty shell and would waste away in days."

"How - how could you have been so sure? What if you'd been wrong?" Zarah asked.

I cleaned my sword and sheathed it. "If I were wrong, then she'd be dead right now, as would we. I don't dwell on 'what ifs,' only certainties. I was right, and we are alive. That's all that matters."

I wouldn't let Zarah see, but murdering the young girl had shaken me. Regardless if she were possessed, the anguish in her eyes cut me to my soul. At one point, she had been a regular human like any other. I cursed mentally at having forced myself to watch the light fade from her eyes. She deserved that much, but some things would haunt a man's dreams until he died.

Zarah peered out from behind the curtain that led behind the stage. "Look here!"

I pushed the vision of Emlee's eyes from my mind and joined Zarah.

"A storage chest!" Zarah exclaimed. "I found a small bag of supplies as well. She had some dried meat and fruit, as well as two large skins of water."

I looked around the room, which was much larger than I had expected. Unfortunately, it looked as if most of the room was filled with rotted props and dust-covered junk. Had people worshiped in this church in the past? Who had they been? Emlee's last words indicated at least some of the ghouls had been trapped people like us.

Zarah uncoiled a small bit of rope. "Let me see your knife."

She sliced off several strands from the rope and tied them together to form a string. She put the end of the string in her mouth and smoothed it down and then cautiously threaded it through the keyhole of the chest. She wound it around my knife and inserted its tip gently into the opening. She motioned me back and turned her head before tugging on the string. The knife twisted slightly, resulting in an audible *click*. A puff of dust jetted from a hole to the left of the lock mechanism.

Zarah chuckled. "I suppose whatever poison had been in the trap has long since evaporated, but better safe than sorry."

"You're a master thief, too?"

"Let's just say I've had to pick a few locks in the past. Traveling around and performing in shady inns puts you in contact with some interesting characters."

"You're a woman of many talents."

She smiled slyly at that comment but didn't take the obvious bait with a follow up wisecrack. Instead, she focused on picking the lock. "What I'd give for a proper lock pick." Finally, the lock clicked, and she opened the chest.

She peered into the chest and shouted with glee.

"What is it? More gems? Gold?"

"Something much better!" She exclaimed before pulling out her prize. "Shoes!"

CHAPTER FOURTEEN
Shopping

"They're too large, but I'm not picky," Zarah said as she pulled the knee-length leather boots on.

The rest of the chest contained various mementos and knickknacks looted from the few adventurers who had made it this deep into the dungeon. At the bottom of the chest, I found a few gold coins and added them to the others. A bible devoted to Castigous contained two parchments. I studied them for long moments before realizing they were related to the summoning sigils.

Zarah looked at me with curiosity. "Anything worthwhile?"

I continued to study the fascinating theorems laid out on the parchments. "These are far more advanced than my current understanding of magic, but theoretically I could learn summoning magic from them. This helps explain how she was able to set up the summoning circles around this level. It's very difficult magic."

Zarah looked around the room. "Can it summon us out of this place?"

"That's not how summoning works. You place something into a temporal void then summon it back later. Whereas a necromancer might animate a skeleton, a summoner must first store something into a state of suspension. Then he can summon it later. Such as a dagger or food."

"That doesn't sound very impressive. I've seen magic pouches that can store large things like that."

"Yes, but a summoner can place living creatures or even spells into a temporal void. I believe that wraith stored these people's life force into these sigils and could release it under her control whenever she wished."

"It doesn't seem very helpful in our current predicament," Zarah said as she looked behind a curtain only to find a stone wall. "I think —" she began to say before she paused. She looked down at her foot, which had stepped upon a small rug. She stomped several times before looking up, a smile on her face. She whipped away the rug, revealing a trap door.

"I knew there was something here."

I joined her and inspected the hidden door. A metal rung rested in an indention in the wood so that it would not protrude past the flat surface. "And how did you know that?"

"Bard's intuition. Sometimes an expedient exit from a dire situation is warranted."

I stuck the summoning parchments into my spellbook and stowed it before lifting the metal ring and opening the doorway. A ladder led down into darkness.

I closed the trap door and thought about our situation. Was going deeper into the structure the wisest decision? Each level brought new dangers and foes. Aside from Zarah, the entire population thus far had been hostile. The wraith had been correct — we did not possess a weapon capable of harming mystical entities. Only a blessed or enchanted weapon could affect such beings. I wasn't sure why the wraith had collapsed. Perhaps the shock of having her mortal vessel destroyed, coupled with the huge drain on her caused by summoning so many ghouls? Either way, we'd been fortunate.

Zarah placed her hand gently on my arm. "Why are you hesitating?"

"I was just weighing our options. It seems the creatures become more powerful as we venture deeper. We may not be equipped to deal with what may come."

"So, we're going to remain on this floor? What if she returns? We don't know how long she'll be gone."

I looked out through the curtains at the collapsed zombies. "True. She could be gone minutes or years. Our alternatives are back to the goblins or down. We can't remain here."

Zarah opened our supplies and handed me some food and water. She looked in the bag. "With Emlee's supplies, we should have a few days' worth of food and water. I was getting concerned because what we'd stolen from the torturer was getting low."

"Yes, I suppose one advantage that these floors are all inhabited is the creatures who dwell here must eat and drink as well, so finding supplies may not be as difficult as I'd first thought."

"As long as we aren't on the menu," Zarah said.

We finished our impromptu meal and packed our supplies. I reopened the trapdoor and began to descend but almost lost my grip.

"Careful!" Zarah said as she offered me her hand.

I waved it away. "It's nothing. My arms are a bit weak from the battle with the ghouls. We need to rest, but it's too dangerous at the moment. When I get to the bottom, I'll block the orb's light three times to signal it is safe." I continued down. The glowing orb of light descended into the passage and moved down below my feet. "Useful," I whispered. It seemed the orb now moved to where I looked and needed the most light rather than remaining in a static position.

The ladder was made of thick iron covered in a layer of rust. It was solid enough, but I motioned for Zarah to wait until I called for her. The space around the ladder was larger than expected. Someone twice my size could easily fit. It made me wonder what waited below. The magical orb paused as my foot struck the floor. I looked back up only to see a small square of light from Zarah's torch.

The small room I'd entered was empty. A solitary door blocked the entrance. I signaled for Zarah and remained on guard in case the door opened. Her torch tumbled down the shaft and clattered on the ground. She joined me minutes later, slightly out of breath. "Perhaps we should carry fewer supplies."

I signaled for her to be silent and listened. Someone was approaching. The door swung inward. A small humanoid entered. I readied my sword, but he made no threatening movements.

"Greetings," he said. Our visitor was three feet tall and wore the garb of a merchant. Massive metallic-and-glass goggles sat atop his head. He wore a leather apron adorned with pouches and pockets. His fiery red hair erupted between the goggle's tight band around his head and almost appeared to glow. His green eyes twinkled as he offered a smile.

Speechless, I finally recovered from the initial surprise. "H-hello."

"And who might you be?" he asked.

I wasn't convinced this wasn't a trap of some kind, so I kept my distance. "You reveal your name and purpose first, friend."

He chuckled. "My name is Quinley Goldgild."

"What's a gnome doing in a place like this?" Zarah asked.

"What's a beauty like *you* doing in a place like this?" he responded. I swear Zarah blushed.

"I'm Zarah Telon, and my companion can't seem to remember his name at the moment, but you can call him Hero."

Quinley looked me up and down before nodding his approval. "Aye. He appears to be a hero of some kind, albeit it one with poor fashion taste. A hero must look the part, lad! You look like you robbed clothes from a housewife's clothesline."

I looked at my mismatched outfit and felt a slight twinge of embarrassment. "Yes, well, I started with merely a loincloth and ragged pants. We are trying to find a way out of this place. Are you trapped here as well?" He seemed harmless, but so had Emlee. If he'd ventured this deep into the dungeon, had he done it on his own? He had no weapons or companions.

Quinley rubbed his hands together vigorously. "Nay, I'm here to offer you useful items that may help you on your way!"

"Pardon me, but you seem to have forgotten your items at home," Zarah said as she looked him over. "Unless they are in those small pockets and pouches of yours. Do you have a magical pouch with a few baubles in it?"

Quinley burst out laughing so hard, he doubled over. A minute later, he had to wipe the tears from his eyes and catch his breath. "Oh, beautiful lass, you're an observant one, you are. Nay, I've brought my store for you to peruse."

My smile quickly turned into a frown. Apparently, we'd found a mentally ill wanderer who had somehow managed to remain alive within the deadly confines of the dungeon. Perhaps he'd been tortured and lost his mind from the constant agony.

"Nay, I'm not daft," Quinley said as he rifled through the large pocket on the front of his apron.

Startled, I wondered if he'd heard my thoughts or had merely guessed what we were thinking. There could be more to this small man than we'd assumed.

Zarah played along with his outlandish suggestion. "By all means, let's see what you have to offer, Mr. Goldgild." She looked around the empty room, mimicking a trip through a store. She grabbed an invisible item and inspected it. "Exquisite quality, I must say."

Quinley burst out laughing yet again. "Oh, I like you two! You're not all dour and dark like most of my customers! No, step into my actual shop!" He pulled out a small object from his pocket and showed it to us. It was a miniature door. He held up a finger and motioned for us to step back as he placed the door on the ground. He tapped the door with a key held in his other hand. Instantly, the door expanded to normal size.

"Amazing..." I murmured as I attempted to analyze what type of magic he was using. Was the door magical or was the key? Perhaps they were both part of the spell. After my initial shock wore off, I was confronted by the fact that we stood in front of a wooden door which led to nowhere. The novelty had worn off.

Again, Quinley motioned for us to wait as he gently inserted the key into the door's lock. With an audible click, the tumblers turned. The excited gnome motioned for Zarah to open the door.

"Oh, this is the way to your shop?" Zarah said, still playing along. She turned the knob and the door opened. She gasped.

"What in the name of Theala..." she muttered as she peered into the impossible.

The doorway led into what could only be described as a large shop far bigger than the room we occupied. The walls were lined with various armors, suits, and weapons while racks of clothes filled the middle aisles. On the right side of the room, bookcases overflowed with books of all shapes and sizes. On the left, potions and bottles covered every inch of the shelving. Scents of metal, oil, food, spices, and dozens of others flooded into the room along with warmth emitted by a giant stone hearth on the far side of the room.

The room itself looked incredibly sturdy, with giant wood beams holding up the massive walls. In the far corner, a suit of armor crafted for a giant almost touched the huge domed ceiling, which rose at least fifty feet into the air. There must have been thousands of items in the shop.

"This...is inexplicably powerful magic," I said as I cautiously looked through the doorway, careful not to enter. The enticing room could be a trap — perhaps an illusion meant to lure us into imprisonment or worse.

Quinley stepped through the doorway and stamped on the wooden floor. "It's real. Not a trick. C'mon in! I've got a pot of stew on the hearth that I offer to all first-time customers. If you buy something, I'll even throw in a pitcher of my third-best mead!" He skipped away as if thrilled to have visitors.

Walking to the other side of the door, I was surprised to see nothing but an ordinary wood surface. Cautiously, I reached out to touch it.

"Should we go with him? That stew smells very good," Zarah whispered.

I touched my chin and stroked it. "Why would a gnome be wandering a dungeon selling his wares? He'd have much more luck in a marketplace. This is illogical."

Zarah opened up a pouch, which contained the gold and gems we'd found from the previous levels. "Dungeons of lore are filled with treasure, are they not? So perhaps this fellow waits for adventurers to find the treasure, then he offers his services."

"With magic this powerful, he should be able to overcome just about any creatures he encounters with ease. His shop is filled with wands, weapons, spellbooks...he doesn't need anyone to find treasure for him."

"Does he look like a warrior to you?" she asked.

I watched him joyfully arranging a meal for us as he doled out ladles of stew into large wooden bowls. She could have a point — why risk your own neck when someone else has done the work for you? That still didn't explain how he'd come to be where we were. Entering the shop, I was wary. "Be on guard and signal if you see anything suspicious," I whispered over my shoulder. Zarah was already browsing the wares. I noticed my globe of light remained outside as if waiting for us to return. Curious.

Quinley motioned for us to join him at a large table. "My friends, come join me for a drink and a bite."

We sat with the gnome and surveyed the meal in front of us. Lifting the spoon, I cautiously sniffed the stew.

The gnome stuffed his mouth with a spoonful of the delicious-smelling food. "Come, come, it's not poisoned!"

I lifted the spoon to my mouth but paused. "May I ask about the ingredients of this delicacy?"

Quinley gulped down a mouthful before proudly boasting, "Tender venison, sweet carrots, potatoes, wild onions, and just a pinch of my special spices. Can't tell you the last part because I swore to my grandmother I'd take it to my grave."

Taking a sip, I didn't notice anything unusual. There were potent poisons that had no scent or taste, but if he was eating it himself, I doubted he'd have an immunity to such deadly chemicals. Finishing my spoonful, my taste buds ignited with flavor. Quinley was a phenomenal chef.

"This stew is the best I've ever had — and I've had a lot of stew in my life," Zarah said.

"Oh, lass, you're a bit too kind. Thank you for the praise."

The mead matched the stew's robust and hearty flavor. Before I knew it, my bowl and mug were both empty.

Quinley leaned over the table and inspected my empty bowl. "You'd like another? The first sampling is free, but the second will cost you!"

I looked to Zarah. Was this where he sprung his trap? My hand moved to my sword's hilt.

"Two silver! One for each of you, and that includes another round of mead," Quinley said.

I removed my hand, feeling slightly foolish for suspecting him. Zarah fished out a gold coin and handed it to the small man. He looked it over then fished out eight silver. He then gathered our bowls and mugs and returned shortly with refills.

Zarah took a long swig of mead and wiped her mouth with her arm. "Why would a shopkeeper sell food to customers? Shouldn't you have a barmaid or someone around for that?"

Quinley looked hurt. "Then I'd have to share my profit! This way I keep every copper I make. I also like mingling with my customers. What's the point of being in the business of selling things if you don't like people? That's half the fun!"

I looked around the room as I chewed the delectable meal. In addition to his regular wares, the walls and floors were decorated with animal skins and heads. Some of which I'd never seen before — or at least remembered seeing. It then struck me that the room contained windows. We were out of the dungeon!

I leapt from my stool. "Where are we?"

Quinley looked to Zarah, but she merely shrugged. "We're in my shop, my friend. There's no reason to be alarmed. Did you hit your head before I met up with you?"

"No, I mean what town or city is this? Where is your shop located?"

A look of knowing crossed Quinley's face. "Ah, so that's your question. You think we've teleported out of the place you were and are somewhere else. Nay, we are still in that nasty dungeon. We haven't gone anywhere. I'm merely here to sell or buy, not rescue you."

"What do you mean? This store can't fit in that room. We can't logically be where we were!" I said.

"Have a look for yourself, friend," Quinley said as he motioned toward a window.

I rushed to the nearest set of drapes, pulled them aside, and gasped. Indeed, the view was of the room we'd just come from.

"This...makes no sense," I said. The orb of light peeked around the corner. It was apparently following me on the other side.

Quinley laughed. "Many things in this world make no sense! There are pouches that can hold armor and weapons, but you're amazed by this?"

"You know this is a completely different principle. The space in magicked pouches is uninhabitable by any living thing. This room contains light and warmth. I assume it is a pocket dimension?"

Quinley raised an eyebrow. "Oh, a pocket dimension? Where'd you learn about such things?"

"I...wish I knew. I have knowledge, except of myself."

The small man took a large swig of mead and wiped his mouth with his sleeve. "That's an interesting dilemma. Most people know only about themselves and their petty little lives, and care not for the world, history, science, or magic."

"It's not by choice, I can assure you," I said as I let the drapes fall back into place. For a brief moment, it had seemed the nightmare was over.

"Sorry for your predicament, but you're in luck — you've met me. Now, for the main event. Feel free to browse my wares. Just ask me if you need to know how much I'm asking for the item."

Zarah opened her pouch and showed our gems to Quinley. "How much do you value these?"

Quinley lowered his goggles. Using his finger, he flipped several small gears on the side, which resulted in an audible click within the goggles. "Not bad pieces. Clarity and cut could be better, but they're of decent size. I'd say about two-hundred gold."

Zarah's eyes lit up, but she said nothing. She drew me to the side, out of his range of hearing. "This gnome is crazy. Those gems are worth maybe twenty-five gold, don't you agree?"

While I thought his estimate was slightly on the high side, Zarah's estimation was insane, but I decided to let it pass. "How much gold do we have without the gems?"

"Thirty-one, and ten silver," she answered.

"We should be able to buy quite a bit with that," I said as I looked around the room.

"Do you have a —" I began to ask, but Quinley interrupted me and whipped out a leather bag.

"Satchel of Storing?"

I inspected the bag. It was very well made. "How'd you know..."

"It doesn't take a genius to realize you're both overladen with items. Almost every adventurer's first purchase is an enchanted bag."

"How much?"

A wicked grin crossed Quinley's face. "Only seventy-five gold."

"Seventy-five?" Zarah practically shouted.

Now I understood. This was the moment Quinley had been waiting for — the haggle. While making money was his prime objective, he reveled in feeling as if he'd outwitted his opponent. It was all a game of wits to him.

I shook my head. "I had no idea these prices were so high. I suppose you enjoy taking advantage of desperate adventurers, but we are not so desperate as to blow almost one-third of our budget on a bag. Your offer is insulting!" I rose and gathered our items before heading toward the door. "Come along, Zarah."

"But...aren't we..." Zarah said as she looked desperately around the room. She quickly scooped up her items and followed.

Quinley rushed to get in front of us. "Wait, you're just going to leave? I have magical items, food, water, weapons, and armor, and you'll just leave that behind?"

"I know your type — one that waits for a fire or flood and then raises his rates to deprive destitute families of their entire wealth. An immoral, unscrupulous blackguard who would take us for all we have and leave us with shoddy trinkets!" I said in a condemning tone as I moved around him. "No, thank you. I won't be fooled by false shows of kindness to lower my defenses. Thank you for the mead and stew and good day to you, sir!"

Quinley trotted behind us. "You won't even consider my wares? Prices *do* have some flexibility to them."

"Your initial offer demonstrates that your products will be far above our means!" I said as we walked through the doorway and back into the room at the base of the steps. I ventured toward the doorway Quinley had initially come through, hoping Quinley stopped me before I ran out of space. My theatrics would have to end on the other side of the doorway, as I'd have to be cautious to avoid traps or creatures.

Quinley again moved to block my path. "Now, just wait. What if I offered the bag at a discount, just to win you over? Say — fifty gold?"

"Fifty?" I shouted as I looked past him as if judging how far I had to walk to get away from him.

"Forty-five?" the small man asked sheepishly.

"I've seen similar bags for twenty gold in low-end shops," I said.

Quinley grabbed his chest. "T-twenty? I paid more for it, myself! Forty is as low as I'll go. Not a gold lower. If you saw bags that cheap, they were imitations!"

I looked down at him and held out my hand. "Deal." In reality, I didn't have any memories of shopping, but I merely assumed he'd be willing to take a significant amount less.

He looked surprised at my sudden change in demeanor but smiled as he held his hand out. "Oh, this is going to be a challenge, I can see."

We spent the next few hours browsing hundreds of items in the shop. Unfortunately, most items were priced far beyond our meager means. A few gems and gold didn't go far in Goldgild's Bizarre Bazaar. We left with adventuring outfits that actually fit properly, made of sturdy materials that would provide protection from chaffing from the leather armor we wore.

We had the Satchel of Storing, and gained five days' worth of food, water, and a bottle of wine. I also managed to talk Quinley down on a lightly enchanted Dagger of Cold in case we encountered any more enchanted creatures. Its enchantment had faded over time until it was almost gone, but it would have cost more to recharge it than the shoddy weapon was worth. It wouldn't do much more damage than a normal dagger, but it was better than nothing. I bought several blank parchments and an enchanted quill which could write for days without needing ink. Zarah had complained for ten minutes straight about how much the quill had cost, but I had some magical theorems and notes I wanted to put to paper as we explored.

Zarah purchased a leather vest so that she had some protection for any future combat encounters. Quinley's shoe selection wasn't much better than the over-sized leather boots she'd just gained, so she decided to keep what she was wearing. Her eyes lit up when she found a simple bronze flute in a bin of marked-down items. It was slightly bent but functioned. Quinley let the musical instrument go for a mere silver.

Exhausted, we bid farewell to the merchant and exited his store. The orb of light had long-since faded. As Quinley said his final goodbye, he closed the door, plunging us into darkness. I used the firesparker and fumbled for a torch. I cursed as I'd forgotten to purchase more. My light spell was a fine replacement, but you never knew when a fiery torch would come in handy.

"Quinley, do you have..." I began to say, but Zarah touched my arm and pointed.

"He's gone."

Indeed, the wooden doorway had disappeared as soon as it had closed. We were completely alone again.

CHAPTER FIFTEEN
Onward

We decided our current room would suffice well enough for the night. It was impossible to discern the time, but it was most likely approaching dusk. The fight on the previous floor and our exploration of the church had to have been close to half a day, and we'd spent almost to three-quarters of that with Quinley. After getting only a partial night's sleep and fighting our way through the ghouls, we were both exhausted.

We rigged a basic noise-making trap on the door using my old dagger and some of the rope. If the door opened, we'd know.

Zarah pulled out our makeshift bedding from the satchel. "I'll never understand how these things work. Only wealthy patrons ever owned them. I never thought I would."

I stripped off my armor. "I never thought I'd be battling for my life in a creature-infested dungeon."

Zarah helped me remove a few pieces. "That Quinley was certainly an odd fellow. What do you suppose he was doing here?"

"I suspect he's some kind of powerful sorcerer who is looking for artifacts of rare power. He certainly seems to enjoy his work, however."

Zarah removed a wineskin from the satchel. "This makes travel easier. I don't know how it always knows which item to retrieve." She gulped down the wine and offered it to me. It was a strong blend, bringing to mind an array of fruits. I tried to envision an orchard, but couldn't bring up a picture of one.

Frustrated, I handed the container back to her and lay down. Zarah began to hum at a low volume. "I'd play my new flute, but who knows what roams these halls?" she whispered.

Her relaxing melody caused my mind to wander before I finally dozed off.

At some point I awoke and relieved myself in the far corner. I felt well rested and clear of mind. Zarah awoke soon after I lit a candle. We ate a quick breakfast which consisted of dried nuts, fruit, and meat before readying ourselves. Zarah used a small stick to pick between her teeth.

"Where'd you come across that?" I asked.

"I paid a few copper for some tar tree twigs. They are fantastic for cleaning your teeth and absorbing odors, even if they taste foul," she said as she offered me a small wooden sliver. I gently cleaned between and across my teeth. She was right about the flavor, but my mouth did feel much cleaner.

"Fighting for our lives, buried beneath the earth, and you are concerned about your breath," I teased.

She broke the used tip off and tossed it to the ground. "I'm a bard. Our looks, smile, and hygiene go a long way toward tips. I can't allow an inconvenient detour to ruin my career."

I slipped back into my armor and gathered my weapons. The padded, properly fitted clothes underneath my armor made movement much more fluid and comfortable. We lit a torch and ventured out, a new orb of light obediently leading the way.

This floor had rough-hewn walls as if carved out of stone by hand. I wondered if the church above marked the end of the professional architecture. It soon became evident that these tunnels formed a labyrinthine network.

"We'll have to be careful — it will be easy to become lost," I said as I marked a wall with my nonmagical knife.

We wandered for another hour, but we encountered no enemies.

"Perhaps this is the end of the road?" Zarah said.

I bent down and touched the floor, feeling its smoothness against my fingertips. "No, I feel as if this level was used to house something specific that was too large for rooms like above. Look at how the stone is worn down as if something large and strong has been dragged over it."

Soon after, we discovered the remains of what had inhabited the tunnels. Fortunately for us, they had been long dead. A long path downward ended in a massive lair that was almost as big as the entire floor above us. Glowing yellow moss hung from the walls and ceiling, creating weak sunlight effect. Vines and other vegetation filled a lush valley where an underground lake awaited. We made our way down a decline as we entered the subterranean forest. Dozens of trees filled the small valley. In a hollowed-out section of the wall, the bones of four large, reptilian creatures remained.

"The remains of some type of drakes," I said as we cautiously approached the den. After studying the bones, I realized this was a remarkable find. "Arbolisks."

Zarah looked around the area as if fearful one of the dangerous creatures would suddenly appear. "I thought they went extinct thousands of years ago."

We crouched down behind a tree and observed the creatures' home, waiting to see if anything moved. Zarah gasped and pointed to the tree we were sheltered under.

The tree's curvy form resembled that of a buxom woman. Her long legs were rooted firmly in the dirt. Her face looked forward in fear, her mouth sealed shut by the same bark that covered her naked body. Her arms rose up high and split into branches. From her base to the top of her upper branches, she was around ten feet tall. The other trees had also been human at some point.

"Exposure to an arbolisk's breath transforms a person into a plant, unable to move, frozen like a statue. This moss must replicate sunlight, or else they would have all withered and died by now," I said as I analyzed the cavern.

Zarah felt across the woman's form before putting her head to the tree's breasts. "I don't detect a heartbeat, and she feels like an ordinary tree."

"Some say they can still hear and feel, even like that. Trapped for perhaps hundreds of years, nothing but living statues."

"A horrible fate..." Zarah said as she backed away.

Satisfied that the creatures were long dead, we proceeded to their den. Shockingly, a large metal door like the ones on the floors above had been built directly into the stone wall on the far side.

"That's a pretty effective deterrent," Zarah said as she studied the giant bones of the dead reptiles. Each skeleton was close to twenty feet in length. Despite their large size and stubby legs, they could move faster than most humans. The fierce predators could shoot a jet of gas from their mouths for a distance of twenty feet. Their chitinous bark-like scales and thick skin were similar to dense trees. Even a stout axe would require multiple strong blows to one spot to reach a vital organ. While fire proved to be partially effective against them, getting them to burn was like getting a lush, green, healthy tree to catch light.

"Oh..." Zarah gasped as she pointed to the far wall of the den. There, in the middle of a dirt mound stood an unusual tree. It was two-feet wide, with scaly, green bark. The main trunk did not branch until it reached the top, which was close to fifteen feet high, where three identical limbs split, all evenly spaced apart. The limbs bowed down toward the ground, but the tips remained five feet in the air. Three unusual fruit, the size of a small watermelon, hung from each branch. They glistened like deep blue, oblong pearls.

I moved closer and began inspecting them. "Eggs."

"They're beautiful," Zarah said as she noticed her distorted reflection on the bottom of one. "Do you think they're still alive?"

Putting my ear to the side of the lizard egg, I listened. "I believe I detect a very faint, low murmur. It could be a heartbeat."

Zarah gently touched one of the eggs. "What are you going to do? What if they hatch?"

"These are a rare breed of specimen that was thought to be extinct. We'll leave them be and perhaps the species can rebound one day."

"I...see," she said as she turned away.

Her reaction was puzzling. "You want me to kill them?"

"No, I'm just...surprised by your answer."

"Removing a predator species from the world rarely results in a positive outcome. Look at when we wiped out the cyclops and the drake population exploded. Whole towns were wiped out."

"Yet those people are nothing but trees now because of these creatures. They are dangerous."

"We can't exterminate every creature that is dangerous to us. Besides, who knows what secrets these creatures possess. No one has done an in-depth analysis of their makeup. We don't even quite understand how the animal-to-plant transformation process —"

Zarah walked toward the door and peered through the bars. "Your thirst for knowledge could be your undoing. Many great sorcerers and scientists have died from their pursuits."

"And our knowledge was advanced from their sacrifices. If no one ventured into the world, where would we be now?"

She stared at me for a moment before turning away. "Do you think that lake is safe to swim in? I would kill for a bath."

"I - er, let me inspect it," I said as I joined her. What had that discussion been about? It seemed pointless.

At the water's edge, I knelt and scooped up a sample in my hand and sniffed it. Holding it up to the orb of light, I inspected it closely before letting it run through my fingers. "This water is remarkably clear. It must be fed by an underground stream. I believe it's safe to bathe in and even drink."

"Fortunately, we have a good supply of water from Quinley, so I'll forgo sampling it," Zarah said as she removed her clothes and waded in.

I looked out over the dark, still water. "I'd stay close to shore, however. Everything in this place seems hostile."

Zarah dunked her head under the water before bursting upward, flinging water through the air with her long locks. "Don't worry, I have no intention of swimming out. I merely want to wash the muck and grime away and refresh myself."

I stared at her beautiful form for a moment before turning back to the arbolisk den. Strangely enough, despite her admonition of being filthy, I couldn't recall smelling her during our journey. I shrugged and looked around the area for the missing key. Even if the current floor was safe, we'd need to eventually proceed down.

Sitting on a large bone, I looked out over the eerie forest of human trees and shivered. Something had set my nerves on edge. I pulled out my spellbook and began studying it.

"That was refreshing," Zarah said.

She'd gotten dressed and began drying her hair. "Done so soon? I thought you'd have taken your time," I said.

She looked puzzled. "You get so absorbed in that book. I was gone for almost an hour." She began unpacking a light lunch.

"I find these theorems to be fascinating. I wish I'd had money to buy one of the other spellbooks from Quinley," I said as I gently closed the book.

Zarah took a bite of hard bread. "Have you learned anything useful?"

"Ignatous Fragmentum!" I said as I made a simple sign in the air. A small flaming dart launched from the palm of my hand and impacted the wall, leaving a burned and smoking crater.

Zarah stood and moved to inspect the damage to the wall. "That's quite an improvement!"

"By changing the element, I can launch darts of flame, ice, or magnetic energy," I said.

Zarah motioned to a spot on the wall. "Let me see."

"No. These cost me a lot of spell energy to cast."

"You seem to be able to keep this light spell going continuously," she said.

"Yes. My reserves have increased each day. The key is becoming attuned to the spell through practice and building up a large pool of magical energy. The more I cast, the more of a pool I can develop. Eventually, a spell like this will be less effort than blinking an eye, and I won't even need the sigils for some spells."

"Doesn't it seem unusual?" Zarah asked.

"What?"

"That your abilities are improving this quickly. Is it normal to learn spells this fast?"

"I...don't believe so. I've wondered that myself. Perhaps I have some latent talent for the mystical arts. Or..."

"What?"

"Or perhaps I was already adept at magic before I lost my memory, and I'm just regaining my skills."

"You're regaining more than that. Have you noticed how much stronger you've become since we've met? Your muscles have perceptively grown just in the past few days."

"I'm merely regaining my strength from proper rest and diet," I said, although I knew she was right. Food and sleep couldn't account for my surge in physical strength and magical aptitude. As illogical as it might seem, this place was somehow changing me. At first, I thought it was my imagination, but over time, it became readily apparent. It was both thrilling and terrifying at the same time.

Zarah sat on one of the arbolisk skulls. "Should we look for the key?"

"I've noticed something that may help with that." I stood and approached the door. "Desicry Arcenarum!" A light-green glow ran around the edges of the door. "I believe these keyed doors are magically linked to a specific key." I pulled out the keys to the previous doors. They each glowed with a different color.

"It probably makes picking the lock or destroying the door very difficult," I said as I inspected the door.

Zarah bent down and looked at the lock. "That's not exactly reassuring news. We don't have the key, and now we know getting through the door is impossible. These tunnels are larger than all the other floors combined, and the floor of this cave is covered with vegetation and leaves. How will we find a small key in the midst of all that?"

I pointed to a small wisp of green that floated away from the door. "The key is attuned to this door. That trail means the key is in that direction."

Zarah squinted and tried to follow the faint magic but gave up after a few feet. "I suppose it's better than having nothing to go on. At least we've narrowed it down to one direction. Should we look for it now?"

"I'd like to jot down some notes concerning these eggs and drawings of the skeletal structure of these deceased arbolisks," I said.

Zarah handed me a parchment and the magic quill. "I'm not going to bring it up again, but in a room full of magical weapons and armor, you felt the need to buy that."

"But you just did bring it up," I said as I started sketching the tree and its uncanny 'fruit.'

Zarah set the torch between us so as to provide a bit of warmth and light that we could share. "I'd gather up some wood, but the thought of burning it turns my stomach."

"I'm sure they wouldn't mind," I said as I nodded toward the forest.

"No, but I do." She pulled out her flute. "I think I'd go mad if I had to sit here doing nothing while you studied. I can't even explore for fear of running into some horrible beast. Fortunately, it seems we are alone on this level, so..." She began to play a light, whimsical melody.

An hour later, Zarah stopped and stared at her instrument. "It's been so long since I've played a flute. I love how portable it is, yet powerful."

"Do you play any other instruments?" I asked as I finished a final note on the egg-tree.

"Every instrument," she replied. "I may not have mastered them all, but I haven't found one I can't play."

"Every?" I asked, incredulous.

"Once you learn the basics of an instrument, others of its type follow similar methods. I was raised in a traveling troupe of entertainers, so I've been singing, dancing, and playing since my very first memories." She stared into the fire, a look of contentment on her face. I remained quiet and left her to her fond memories.

"Do you recall much of your family?" I asked as I studied a skull.

"Yes. We traveled from town to town, singing and dancing and entertaining. My grandmother was the comedian of the group. A short, plump old woman who could make even the most dour of people howl with laughter. My father and mother would dance with each other around the campfire at night, mesmerized by each other's eyes. Many local rulers requested their shows. My brother...my brother..."

"What about your brother?" I asked absentmindedly.

Her smile faded. "It's not important. Those were happier times. We traveled the world, ate different foods, learned of new customs while bringing joy and entertainment to people who needed it most."

I stopped and studied her demeanor. She'd stumbled upon troubling memories. "A valiant occupation."

She stood and walked away from me to stare out over the trees and lake. "You really think so? You don't think it's a foolish dream?"

"'Music and art soothe the soul, agitate the imagination, and elevate the mind,'" I replied absently.

Zarah turned around. "Who said that?"

I paused my notes and thought. "I...don't remember. A philosopher, I suppose. But yes — I do believe music and art are very important."

"The light's dimming."

"What? That's illogical," I said as I stepped away from the torch. Indeed, the light in the cavern had dimmed significantly since we had first arrived. "Perhaps the glowing plants are on the same cycle as the sun? Or do their root systems extend to the surface and sunlight itself is transferred deep into the earth?" I said as I studied the ceiling.

"Does it matter?" Zarah laughed. "I was merely pointing out that it's beautiful in here at the moment. We may never see such a sight again for as long as we live."

"I'd rather view the sunset from the surface."

"My grandmother used to say most of your life is spent traveling, so enjoy where you are at the moment."

I noticed a hint of sorrow in Zarah's last statement. "Has she passed?"

She was silent for a long period before replying. "Yes, she's gone." She turned away and wiped tears from her face.

"I'm sorry, I didn't mean..."

"No — it's fine. I'm...fine."

I walked back to our makeshift camp and noticed the torch's light had grown low. Two torches sat in sconces on either side of the door. I'd noticed traces of magic about them when I casted my detect magic spell earlier. I removed them both and stored them, then laid out our bed.

"It's gotten a bit dirty, hasn't it?" Zarah said, pointing to the dingy cloth.

"Still the better alternative to the floor," I said as I stretched out.

Zarah sat down. "That bath was extremely refreshing."

"I'm glad you had the opportunity to cleanse yourself," I replied as I looked over my notes. "Did you know these bones actually seem to be mostly a form of partially petrified wood? They are nothing like the bones of other animals. Of course, they've dried out over time, which seems to have made them more brittle."

"That's fascinating. Perhaps we could wash these blankets before we pack them away tomorrow. Might as well take advantage of the lake while we're here."

I rolled up the parchment. "Are you trying to tell me something?"

"You stink. Go take a bath, please," Zarah laughed.

CHAPTER SIXTEEN
Tangled

After a small breakfast the next morning, we refilled our water skins at the lake. We weren't low, but there was no way of predicting when we'd next have a chance to do so. We'd learned from previous encounters to pack our things in case we needed to make a hasty exit and to only unpack what was necessary for the moment. We then set out to find the key.

The vines and plants slowly brightened over the next hour, simulating a sunrise. The difference was the whole cavern illuminated evenly at the same time, so there were no long shadows that stretched and swayed as the sun moved across the sky.

We hiked back up the winding slope and headed for the far side, which branched off into various tunnels. Zarah's keen eyes swept across every surface, looking not only for the key, but also traps. Periodically, I used the detect magic spell just in case a hidden room or area contained the key, making sure to mark the area so I wouldn't waste magic in the same spot twice.

After one particularly winding subsection of tunnel, a small cubbyhole split off. Inside, we discovered the bones of an adventurer. It was impossible to determine the corpse's gender or identity, but a metal round shield laid covered by a layer of dirt not far from the body. The shield's leather straps had stiffened with age but hadn't rotted away.

I cleaned the shield's surface and was surprised to see gleaming metal below the dirt instead of rust. A rainbow of colors shimmered as I tilted it.

Zarah leaned in to get a better look. "What's it made of?"

"I believe it's chromatic steel. You can tell from the colors that dance across its surface. The method of making it was lost long ago."

"Is it magical?"

"No. It has powdered crystals that are mixed in with the metal as it's forged. It gives it resistance to water and the elements. It's slightly more durable than regular steel, but there is nothing magical about it." Just in case, I cast detect magic, but I was right. It was a normal shield, although a beautiful piece of craftsmanship. I worked the leather back and forth a bit to loosen the stiffness and strapped it across my back. "I'll need lanolin or something similar to fully recondition it. This will make up for my lost spear. If I'm to give up range, at least I'll be protected in close combat."

"I just see more weight to be lugged around," Zarah griped.

We continued searching, but after three hours, we'd retraced our steps and were back to the edge of the valley.

Zarah frowned. "Perhaps your magic was wrong?"

I wiped the sweat from my brow. The cave system seemed to become somewhat humid during the day despite the lack of direct sunlight. "No, there's one place we haven't looked." I pointed straight down to the lake.

"You can't cast your spell underwater. How will you find a key in all that water? Crawl around on the bottom?"

"I'll swim out and cast. Hopefully the spell will reach deep enough to illuminate the key."

"And if it doesn't?"

"Then we'll have to crawl around on the bottom."

I stripped down to my undergarment, setting my armor, clothing, and gear on the shore on the left side of the lake. "I'll start here and work my way across by going back and forth. It's a simple process of elimination." Wading out, I was surprised when the ground abruptly dropped off. I hoped the lake wasn't too deep, or the key could be lost forever.

"I'll guard our things while you're gone," Zarah said as she warily eyed the frozen tree people that lurked nearby.

"Hopefully there's nothing to guard them against," I said as I swam out a bit. "Try and use those eagle eyes of yours to see what I can't." Casting detect magic, I spun about in the water but saw nothing. I moved out farther and repeated the process. Zarah walked up the ramp and looked down from above but said nothing.

After twenty minutes, I returned to shore. I'd covered about one-fifth of the lake but had become fatigued from both the physical exertion and the action of casting the spell repeatedly. I was pumping more magical energy into the spell, making it the equivalent to a level-two spell. It extended the range but also drained my magical stamina faster.

Zarah and I met near where I'd first entered the water. Winded, I sat on the lush forest floor. She passed out some food and sat beside me. "I'm tired just watching you."

"Although my physical strength and magical reserves have increased, apparently my endurance could use some work," I said as I gnawed on the edge of a piece of bread. "I miss Quinley's stew already."

Zarah looked out over the water. "Do you think there are any fish in the lake?"

"I've seen a few albino fish swimming about. They seem to be blind. Perhaps they originated from an area where there is total darkness and found their way through underground rivers to the lake. Or perhaps the plant growth came about later in their evolution, adding light to the cave."

She laughed. "Must everything be figured out?"

"I'm intrigued by this place. Its layout and structure make no sense. The jail and torture chambers fit together, but why a floor guarded by goblins? A church...now this cave system and lake. The deeper we go, the less logical it becomes."

"There are tales of legendary dungeons of power where adventurers go to find ancient relics, weapons, and to test their mettle against legions of foes. Each floor could be a realm of ice or a swamp...or a forest."

I smiled. "One of your fanciful bard stories? Those old fairy tales were popular hundreds of years ago. Made popular by *The Five Follies*, a book by the scribe Ehryon."

"No, I've known warriors who have returned from these dungeons. They are powerful heroes, made stronger through their battles within these places. Just as you are becoming."

It sounded like superstition. "What about yourself? If surviving this place changes a person, why aren't you?"

She retrieved her flute. "Who says I'm not?" She began playing a slow, sad melody that picked up its pace. Her rhythm increased and she changed the tune to the one she'd hummed during our battle with the ghouls. Suddenly, the veins on my arms bulged, and I felt my strength returning...no, increasing. The song's power had been magnified.

She paused. "I'm twisting two melodies together. One provides a boost to strength, the other to increase endurance. The instrument improves the power of the song, but my musical skill has also increased."

"There's obviously a mystical component to your music. You've trained in magic?"

"Music is its own magic. Once you reach a certain level of skill, it can create miracles. Hate, strength, pain...even love."

"I think there's more to it than that. Perhaps if we ever escape this place, we could study it together."

Zarah smiled. "Oh, you don't know what you're getting into."

My heart raced at her suggestion. "I'd just like to know more about you — I mean, your abilities." The images of her descending into the lake barged into my mind. She was a beautiful woman, but surviving this torturous dungeon had been at the forefront of my thoughts until now.

"If we escape this place, I'll be more than happy to let you treat me to the most fabulous meal either of us have ever had," she said. "I know some of the best taverns in all the land."

"I'd...like that," I said as I stood and stretched. "There's no reason to let the effects of your songs go to waste." I waded back into the water, now filled with something other than dread. I hoped it wouldn't prove to be a distraction.

The effects of her music wore off five minutes later, but I still felt well rested. Perhaps they had rejuvenated my body in addition to providing a temporary boost. I moved closer to shore and cast my spell again.

Zarah called out from up high. "There! To your right!"

I twisted in the water and looked down. The reflections of the glowing plants above us made it hard to see. I dove under the water and saw a faint glow deep down. Excited, I broke the surface and took several breaths before flipping downward and swimming toward the glow. I prayed it was a key and not a useless magical trinket.

As I descended deeper, the water became darker and colder. Fear crept into the edges of my consciousness. Within fifteen feet of the object, I thought I could make out the shape of a key, but my lungs were aching. I turned around and kicked for the surface. The object was deeper than I'd estimated. Bursting out of the water, I gasped for air.

Zarah called out from the far shore while she made her way back around the edge of the lake. "Is it the key?"

"I...believe so," I shouted back. My muscles ached. I turned over on my back and floated, allowing my body a chance to rest. The light in the cave had begun to dim again. I would probably only get one or two more chances before it was dark. Even if the key glowed, I didn't want to be fumbling around in utter darkness trying to determine which direction led to the surface.

Having recovered, I took several long breaths and slowed my heartbeat before descending again. The trip down this time was noticeably darker. My first instinct was to swim harder so that I would reach the object faster, but I calmly continued, using slow, measured strokes.

The glowing item slowly faded into view — it was a key. My lungs began to burn again, but I ignored the pain and continued down. My first grab missed, but the second scooped up the key. Then something moved nearby — something large. I felt the water pressure change and a cloud of sediment erupted, blocking visibility.

Panicking, I flipped over and kicked for the surface. I emerged from the cloud and was relieved to see I was moving in the right direction. I could hear something below me, but it must still be trapped in the cloud. I broke the surface and gasped for air.

"Grab our things! Run to the door!" I shouted. Zarah looked confused for a moment before she realized something was wrong. She stuffed what she could into the satchel and grabbed up my clothing and weapons and raced to the door.

My limbs were numb as I swam for the shore. It felt as if I was moving through quicksand. Behind me, something broke the surface. Zarah looked back and shouted a warning. Against my better judgment, I looked over my shoulder and witnessed a large, reptilian beast swimming toward me — an arbolisk.

My foot finally made contact with the bed of the lake and I trudged up out of the water. Zarah awaited me at the door, but I had the key. Judging by the distance from myself to the creature, and the speed it was moving, I wouldn't make it to her in time. I threw the key toward her and turned to the right, running toward the path that led upward. My legs trembled from swimming for so long. Looking back, I was relieved to see the arbolisk was following me. It was faster in the water than on land, with its short, stubby legs driving its large body forward at a pace that equated to a jog.

It looked similar to other drakes of its type, except for the unusual scale patterns which resembled tree bark. Its dull, gray-green skin sagged against its withered body. This creature was incredibly old and would die soon. Since it was as much a plant as animal, it could probably hibernate underwater for years, soaking in residual light from the plants above while the cool water temperature helped delay the aging process while providing hydration. My thrashing about in the water must have awakened it. If it had been a young specimen, I doubt I could have outrun it.

I looked toward the den. Zarah had retrieved the key and was racing back toward the door. I looped around the outer wall, trying to lead the creature away from her, but also to give myself room to circle back around while outside of the range of its breath weapon.

I reached the path leading back up and considered taking it, but if I got turned around in the myriad of caves, I could easily stumble back upon the creature and have nowhere to flee. Instead, I headed back toward the den. My legs burned and my chest ached. I'd gone straight from swimming, to diving deep into the lake, to running for my life, and my muscles had reached their limit. Twenty feet from the den, my right leg collapsed. I looked up to see Zarah motioning for me to join her at the now-open door, but as she glanced past me a look of fear came over on her face.

I flipped over and shouted, "Ignatous Fragmentum!" just as the arbolisk fired a cloud of green gas toward me. The fiery dart hit the monster's left flank, causing it to roar in pain. I scrambled backward, but the edge of the cloud hit my naked right foot. A numbness flowed into my appendage as the skin darkened.

Shaking, I forced myself back to my feet and hobbled forward. Zarah cried out for me, but I could barely hear her through the roar of blood in my ears. I looked back to see that the enormous lizard had resumed its pursuit. The flame dart had barely caused any damage at all.

A few feet before the den, I tripped and fell forward. Looking down, I could see several slender tendrils had slithered from my foot and taken root into the ground. The arbolisk was almost in range again.

I looked around for a path of escape, but instead saw the torch I'd discarded earlier. It had landed a few feet away from the tree of eggs. "Ignatous Fragmentum! Ignatous Fragmentum!" I shouted as I launched two bolts of fire toward the torch. The first one hit it and reignited it. The other hit the floor a few feet away, kicking up a ball of fire, smoke, and smoldering leaves.

A screech behind me signaled my ploy had worked. The arbolisk stormed past me, toward the tree. I stood with my one good leg and kicked off, wrenching my rooted foot free from the soil. Several roots tore, feeling as if someone had sliced off several of my toes. Zarah met me halfway and helped me to the door. I cast one final glance at the arbolisk before entering the doorway.

Despite the fact that the torch was no real danger to the tree, the beast stomped at the fire until it was out completely. We slammed the door closed, locked it, and made our way down the winding stone steps until I collapsed.

"I-Illuminous Manifestae," I whispered as my body shivered. The familiar orb of light sprang to life, but dimmer and smaller than before. I sweated profusely, both from the physical exertion, but also from the spreading infection on my foot.

"G-get the alcohol," I whispered to Zarah. She looked at me as if I had gone insane. "Hurry!"

She fumbled with the satchel and handed me the bottle. I handed it back to her and shook my head. "T-the s-sparker, too," I said. The skin just below my knee had started to desiccate, turning dark.

"Pour it...on my leg and foot." She did as she was told but looked confused.

"N-now, light it."

"What do you mean? I can't just —" she stammered.

"Light it!" I screamed.

She stepped back and ignited the alcohol with the firesparker. Flames erupted all around my foot and leg, cascading across the bark-like skin. Fortunately, due to the partial numbness caused by the enchanted infection, the pain was dulled. The smell was horrible.

"What now?" Zarah asked in a panic. She held her cloak at the ready.

"W-wait. Just...a little longer," I said. "Now."

She tossed her cloak and patted it down until the fire was out. In an instant, the numbness wore off and the pain hit me. Everything went black.

CHAPTER SEVENTEEN
Past Echoes

I awoke to the sound of music. Zarah played a spry tune on her flute, seemingly lost in thought.

She stopped when she saw me. "Thank Hiala, you're finally awake!" She brought me a water skin, which I gulped greedily from. "Take it easy. You'll get sick if you drink too fast."

"How...long," I asked. My mouth felt as if it was devoid of moisture. After more water, I felt as if I could speak again.

"Almost two days. You've been feverish. I think your body was fighting off the enchantment. That was a mighty stupid thing to do."

I lifted the blanket and looked at my leg. The skin was seared and blackened with bits of burnt bark present in certain areas. "Hand me my dagger."

Picking at the bark, it peeled off, crumbling into ash. It seemed the infection had been removed. "I suspected their breath was a type of contagious magical spore that infected its host. I gambled that fire could purge it before it went too far. Once it made it to my torso, it would have been too late. I'm surprised the damage isn't worse."

"Oh, it was worse. I've been playing a recuperative tune while you were asleep. It speeds up the healing process, but it works very slowly. I'm no cleric, but I figured every little bit helps. I kept it moist with a wet cloth, too." She handed me a bit of dried fruit. "How did you know the beast would protect the eggs?"

"I didn't know for sure. It was a gamble. The torch was too far away to be of any danger to the eggs, but the creature merely saw the fire and reacted to it. Its parental instincts kicked in."

I attempted to stand, but faltered. Zarah helped me to my feet. The room we were in was similar to the one above. Plain stone, no defining features, and a door. I sighed as I limped to the corner to relieve myself.

I returned to Zarah and sat back down. My leg throbbed with pain, causing me to perspire. "Have you explored at all?"

"No, I was afraid to even open the door while you were asleep."

"Any sounds, like a guard or group?"

"No, nothing at all. Maddening silence. I was afraid to light the torches in case I'd use them up. I only lit them when I needed to tend your wounds."

I cast a light spell. The deep bags under Zarah's eyes told me how she'd struggled while I was asleep. "It must have been unsettling, taking care of me, trapped in utter darkness."

"It wasn't so bad. I finally had a bit of peace and quiet from your incessant babbling," she said as she smiled. "Dragging you down the rest of the steps was the hard part."

I touched her hand. "I...very much appreciate it."

She clasped her hand over mine. "We're in this together, whether we like it or not. Besides, you saved me from that pig — the least I could do is save you from a dragon."

I laughed. "That's not quite how I remember it, but we'll just call it even. Do you know how long it will take for your song to fully heal me?"

She frowned. "It's not that strong. You're as healed as you'll get. If I had better instruments and wasn't out of practice, I could do more, but there's no point in continuing. I haven't seen any improvement in the past two hours."

"Do you have an inkling as to what time it is?"

"I'd say evening, but it could be three in the morning. I slept pretty deeply that first night after tending to you."

I lay back and stared up at the ceiling. My body warned me that I needed more rest. As the only capable combatant between the two of us, my leg would prove to be a liability. Zarah began to hum.

"What does this song do?" I asked.

She smiled. "It makes me feel more secure. There's nothing magical about it. Just something I sing when I'm nervous."

I wanted to offer her some words of encouragement, but it wasn't something I was especially good at. It felt like lying. We were in a more dangerous situation, now, and all the platitudes in the world wouldn't change that.

"Are we just going to remain here?" Zarah asked.

"I think I'll be able to move around better tomorrow. I should give my body one more day to rest."

A far-off noise interrupted our conversation. We looked at each other and listened.

I looked up, toward the winding steps. "Was it from above or this level?"

"I couldn't tell."

We set up another rudimentary alarm on the door, using the rope and Zarah's sword. If anything entered, we'd hear. Then we made up our makeshift bed and settled in.

Zarah removed her clothes except for her undergarments. "One of these days, I'll sleep in a proper bed again."

"Yes, I look forward to that as well," I said as I reached for my spellbook. She sighed and sat down beside me.

"Perhaps we could talk a bit, now that you're awake. Please don't bury yourself in that book for the rest of the night."

I closed the book and turned to face her. "I'm afraid I'm not a very good conversationalist. It seems my past is closed to me."

"You can't recall anything of your family or upbringing? A loved one?"

"No. I have access to general knowledge like science and math, but I can't recall anything about myself. Perhaps we could discuss your past."

She looked away. "It's not something I usually talk about."

"Unless you want to discuss my theories on summoning spells or the musculature of the arbolisks, I'm afraid it's up to you. I could use something to take my mind off the throbbing in my leg."

"Well, you know my family traveled about and performed traveling shows all across the country. My father was a handsome man, with long, dark hair and rugged features. My mother's hair was the same color as mine. My father always said I looked like a tiny version of her. Her voice put mine to shame.

There were others in our troupe — Urlo, Magnason, Chae, and his wife and children, my grandmother, my brother."

"What happened to them? Why did you cease to travel with them?" I regretted asking the question as soon as I saw the look on her face.

"We were just outside of a city. I forget which one. We'd had a particularly good haul that day. It was one of our most magnificent performances. My parents were discussing buying a house and settling down. They'd been saving what they could for years. My brother and I argued about what type of house we'd live in." Zarah shook her head and smiled sadly. "Raed thought we were going to live in a castle. I told the idiot we would probably end up in a hovel with a thatch roof, but he always did dream big. Bigger than I ever could." She paused before continuing again.

"As we were preparing for bed, a man entered the camp. He'd overheard my parents talking about the money. Father told him to leave and grabbed his sword but was...struck in the back by a crossbow bolt. Urlo and the others grabbed their weapons, but more men poured into the camp. There were at least ten of them. All well-armed and armored. Even at fourteen, I knew that they were not real bandits.

"My grandmother screamed, and they...slit her throat. I thought of all the tales and jokes she'd told over the years. The merriment she'd brought to thousands. Now silent. They cut down the men and searched our wagons. They stole everything of value, laughing as they ripped up our costumes and smashed our treasured instruments.

"They took the rest of us prisoner. We were tied together and led off through the night to a large estate in the countryside. Duke Merromont's estate. The false bandits secretly worked for him. He was a disgusting man, always drunk and brutal. I recall his rancid smell even now.

"We were enslaved by him for almost a year. He forced my mother and I to...we had to..." Zarah couldn't continue. I wasn't sure how to comfort her, so I just put my hand on her shoulder. She touched it and smiled.

"No, tell me nothing else. I didn't know your past was full of such anguish. I apologize for asking you to tell me of it."

"No, I-I'm not done. I must tell you of Raed. You must know of his sacrifice. One night, one of the Duke's rich friends was visiting and ordered the Duke's guards to bring me to his room. Raed slipped in before the door closed. The man began to beat me, but Raed stabbed him in the back. He kept slicing and stabbing, his face filled with rage. I don't know what was more terrifying — his twisted face or the brutal violence he'd just committed. Raed was always so gentle and innocent. Yet Merromont's cruelty and avarice had crushed that spirit, twisted Raed. We'd been abused and used as cattle, and something that night snapped in my younger brother. His body lived, yet the brother I knew had died.

"He helped me escape. I didn't want to leave my mother behind, but we had no choice. Raed bade me to fetch the local guard and return to help free him and mother. I begged him to come with me, but he said he was the only one who could protect her. Shaking, he held something out for me. It was mother's neckless. As soon as I took it, he ran back toward the estate.

"I ran through the forest, unsure of which way to go, until I saw lights in the distance. I ran for that light. Everything else in the world meant nothing. I don't know how long it took, but I finally arrived. It was the same city we'd performed in almost a year earlier. I begged the guards for help. They shoved me away, but the disturbance brought the Guard Captain. He asked what had happened to me.

"I explained everything that had happened in the past year. The attack on our troupe, our imprisonment, everything. I was in tears and blubbering like a baby by the end of my tale, but at least it was over. The Duke would be brought to justice, and my family would be saved. The large man shook his head in dismay before motioning to his guards. He said Merromont had to be more careful. He'd gotten sloppy. He told them to bring me back to the Duke and bring back twenty gold as compensation for his troubles. I felt all of the strength drain from my body as my hopes were dashed.

"I screamed as the guards grabbed me. One backhanded me, splitting open my lip. A cart arrived and he tossed me in the back before climbing in himself. We set off down the road. The other guard drove the wagon. The one in the back looked me over as if he were a hungry wolf studying a lamb. He asked the one driving if they could delay their visit for a few moments for a bit of fun, but the driver told him it would be unwise to cross Merromont.

"The guard in the back turned to argue, but I slipped in, stole his dagger, and slashed him across the face. He screamed and grabbed for me, but I jumped over the side, tumbling into the road and over the side, which led to a steep ravine. I finally stopped falling, coming to a jumbled halt at the bottom, and then I began running. I could hear the men shouting from up high, but I ran until I could run no more."

"I fled for most of the night until I found my way back to the road. A caravan was heading away from the city, and a woman took pity on me, asking what had happened. I was too afraid to tell her the truth. She seemed to understand and hid me in her wagon. At the next town, she gave me a bit of money and sent me on my way. I believe she probably saved my life.

"I didn't know what to do or who to trust. I began begging, but became fearful of the looks the men were giving me. They were too much like Merromont. I entered a tavern and ate. A bard inside performed for the mute crowd. Despite his talent, the locals weren't being very generous, but he didn't seem to mind. He played for hours. I felt myself humming along, ensnared by his enthusiasm and joviality. Later, he packed up his lute and left. The bar seemed to grow dark and dangerous once he was gone. I caught more than a few eyes upon me. I left and followed him.

"After a while, he paused and, without turning, asked why I was following him. I panicked and hid behind a barrel. When he finally turned, he smiled earnestly and said he recognized me from the tavern and asked if I wanted his money.

"I told him I liked his music and I had nowhere to go. I explained that I was like him and asked if he could help me. He walked back to me and handed me his lute. I played a bit, and he seemed impressed. I told him I was recently orphaned, so he graciously took me under his wing. His name was Faylon, and I'll never forget his generosity. Years earlier, he'd trained to be a combat bard, learning how to enhance his music with magic, but he said the battlefield was no place for people like us. He wanted to bring hope into the world, not warfare.

"He took me on as his student and taught me skills I never knew existed. He said with me in his act, he was earning triple what he'd earned on his own. 'A gleaming face turns a gleaming coin,' he liked to say. I was happy for a time, but I couldn't forgive myself for leaving my family behind. Every day I thought of them more and more. Eventually I told him of them. Faylon initially said there was nothing that could be done, and that I should move on, but he saw how it ate at my soul. One day he vowed to help me get them back." Zarah paused again. This time she couldn't stop the tears.

"He died before he had a chance to keep that promise. I never found out what happened to my family."

I wasn't sure how to respond to such a tale of crushing despair. She'd been carrying this torment with her this entire time, and I hadn't a hint. "I'm...sorry."

She looked up, smiled, and wiped away her tears. "Sometimes the evil ones get away with it, and there's no justice for the good people in the world. I just wanted Merromont to pay for his crimes and to see my brother and mother again."

"Perhaps once we are free of this place, we can find a way," I offered.

She shook her head but seemed defeated. It was as if the fire of her will had burned low. "I'd like to think that's true."

"It's late. You haven't rested properly for days. We'll rest up for the next day or two, then continue exploring."

"What if we never escape? If this just goes deeper and deeper, and more and more monsters come?" Zarah asked as she stretched out on the makeshift bed. "What if we die in this godforsaken place?"

"Then we will die fighting. We can't control our fate, but we've met every challenge and overcame it, and we are both stronger for it."

Zarah curled up beside me. I couldn't help but feel even more responsible for her safety now. I started to hum as the edges of her lips curled into a smile.

Tonight, I would sing her to sleep.

CHAPTER EIGHTEEN
Growing

We spent the next day recuperating. Zarah from her exhaustion and I from my wound. The burn looked worse than it was. Already, some of the burned skin had begun to flake away. The skin underneath looked severely red and had fresh blisters, but the scarring had been kept to a minimum. It still throbbed with pain every second. I thought about imbibing our alcohol to combat the pain, but it had other uses, such as an antibiotic or flammable weapon fuel.

Zarah seemed strangely muted since telling her tale. Was she ashamed? I couldn't read her emotions. Was the lack of sunlight and freedom finally causing cracks in her sanity? Some nights, I felt as if madness had begun to seep into my consciousness. The weight of thousands of tons of rock and dirt bearing down on us, the utter darkness — it would surely drive normal people insane eventually. If not for her company and constant banter, I might have begun to lose my sanity by now. Perhaps I already had. Would I know the difference if I'd started to go mad?

"We have about two more days of food."

"Two?" I said. It seemed we'd bought more than that from Quinley, but perhaps we hadn't been rationing it wisely. "What about water?"

"At least five, maybe more. I refilled our containers in the lake the morning we began searching for the key. I think I left some of the food by the lake during the arbolisk scare. I'm sorry."

We should be able to survive for at least another week or more on what we had, but I was more concerned at the lack of available resources. We couldn't count on another chance encounter with Quinley, and the arbolisk was too dangerous for us to fight with our current equipment. We'd have to press forward and hope to find more supplies or a way out. The underground lake had bolstered my confidence. We could run into an underground stream that led to freedom, although such a proposition was risky.

I continued to study my spellbook while working on some magical formulas. The summoning sigils Emlee had employed could be used in other ways. They worked by storing something within the sigils, then summoning it forth when needed. The drawback of summoning was more magic was needed to store something than was needed to create it, and it cost magic to release it. So, the magical costs were doubled. However, you did not necessarily need to perform motions, draw extra sigils, or chant to cast a spell, and you could set delayed timers or triggers to activate the spells.

I drew a sigil on the ground and imbued it with a hefty portion of magic. Next, I cast the light spell. The orb hovered above the sigil. Focusing, I guided it downward until it touched the glowing symbol on the floor. Slowly, the orb was absorbed into the pattern. Sweat gathered on my forehead as my breathing increased. It had used more magic than I'd estimated.

"Now what?" Zarah asked. I hadn't noticed she'd been watching.

"Now I can summon it again when I need it."

"It won't run out of time while it's in there? Wherever that is?"

"No, I believe it's put into a state of suspension. There are master summoners who are able to summon fantastic beasts. If time passed as normal while they were stored, they'd die from lack of food, water, and possibly air."

"So, go ahead and summon it."

"It's not as easy as it looks," I replied. "Give me a moment."

I slowed my breathing and relaxed, then touched a point on the summoning sigil. The ball of light instantly soared to the ceiling and disappeared into the stone.

"I guess you killed it," Zarah said.

"Perhaps I used a bit more magic than I should have when calling it out. Still, for a twelfth attempt, I believe that was a satisfactory result."

"You've been practicing as I slept?"

"Whenever I can, but not so much as to deplete my reserves."

She sat silently and stared off into space.

"Are you thinking of your family?" I asked.

She looked up and smiled. "It's been so long since I told anyone about that. The only other person who knew the full story was Faylon."

"Can I ask what happened to him? It seems you were close."

She looked as if she was considering it for a moment. "No, that's a tale for another time."

I practiced magic and studied for the rest of the day while she slept on and off.

The next day we had both recovered a bit. Zarah cleaned my leg and changed the bandages she'd put on the previous day. Some of the bandages stuck to the flesh where mucus and pus had soaked them. The intense pain caused me to grit my teeth.

"I don't see any serious infection," she said as she redressed the wound.

"A small miracle," I said as she finished up.

She packed up our things after a light breakfast. My stomach still ached, but we'd decided to start rationing the food. My thoughts flashed back to my starvation when I'd first awoken.

Zarah looked toward the door. "Are we going to continue exploring?"

"Yes. We should rest more, but with our food dwindling, we have to press on. The alternative is to go back up and attempt to kill the arbolisk."

"I'll take my chances on this level. Green is not my color," she said as she checked her gear.

We opened the door and moved into the hall. This floor resembled the upper levels, with walls formed from stone slabs. The first room we came to was a dilapidated storage room. Dust coated the rotten wooden crates.

"Perhaps we'll find some food?" Zarah suggested as she rummaged through some of the debris.

"If we do, I'd be hesitant to eat it," I said as I lifted up a rotted tarp that disintegrated in my hand.

The next room looked like a barracks. "Why would so many troops be stationed in a dungeon, and so deep? It's illogical. They'd have to climb all the other floors in order to be deployed."

"Perhaps this is their deployment. Guarding whatever lies deeper in. A massive treasure could await us."

One bunk on the far end caught my eye. I traveled down and was surprised to find a large lump in the bed, still covered by an old blanket. Zarah joined me and looked shocked when I pointed to the bed. She put her hand on her sword's hilt. I slowly slid my blade out and readied my shield, then motioned for her to pull back the blanket. She frowned — and looked like she was about to protest — but quietly approached the bottom of the bed.

I nodded. She ripped back the blanket and leapt backward. A human-sized skeleton lay in the bed. Its arm tumbled free and clattered on the floor.

"A felae!" Zarah exclaimed.

Indeed, the skeletal structure was slightly different from a human's. Slenderer, with digitigrade feet and clawed fingers. Its head was the most animalistic feature, resembling that of a large cat.

I cast a detect magic spell, but there was no magic present. "I don't believe this one will be chasing us down the halls."

We continued our sweep of the floor. We discovered almost a dozen skeletons, but they'd been stripped of their weapons and gear.

Then we came upon a large decorative room. The room was empty except for a basic throne. After walking and standing for so long, my leg throbbed. I tested the throne's durability and took a seat.

Zarah folded her arms and smirked. "Fancy yourself a leader?"

I slid my hands across the throne's smooth surface. "Simply a tired adventurer." I thought about the floor we were on. It hadn't been occupied by living beings for a hundred years or longer. What were felae doing under the earth? Lush jungles and forests were their natural habitats. What connected the disjointed levels? A prison, a dungeon, barracks, holding cells. Then the church and almost-natural level of the arbolisks stood out as outliers.

Zarah joined me to the right of the throne and began studying it. "What's on your mind?"

"What is the purpose of this place? What happened here? At some point in the past, these levels were occupied. Now they are dead. Who created it and why?"

I turned to observe her. Zarah ran her finger over an emblem at the head of the throne. It was the same symbol that we'd seen outside and inside the church. A man with barbed vines wrapping him tight.

"Now that you point it out, I believe I saw that symbol on something in the goblin chief's room. Perhaps the spine of a book."

"The common theme is Castigous," Zarah said as she pushed the symbol in with her finger. There was a click, followed by the rumbling of stone on stone behind the throne. The button had activated a mechanism which revealed a small alcove that contained a metal chest.

Zarah determined there were no traps and picked the lock. Inside was a strange gleaming silver weapon along with a key. "At least we don't have to scour for the key for a few days," Zarah said as she retrieved both items.

The weapon appeared to be a dagger-like claw attached to a twenty-foot long chain. A silver circlet adorned the other end of the chain. A detect magic spell caused a faint glow to emanate from the strange weapon. I cast the identify spell. It was magical, but it was a weak enchantment that enhanced the weapon's durability and lowered its weight. The enchanter was once again Woll Yaoghun. "The same enchanter as the ring. Perhaps he was imprisoned here and forced to work for the dungeon's masters."

Zarah picked the strange weapon up and admired the craftsmanship. "It's so light. What is it?"

"Not much is known about the felae. They remain fearful and distrustful of humans. I do not recall ever seeing mention of such a weapon." She handed it to me.

I spun it around several times, but the weight seemed off. The clawed dagger ricocheted off the wall, coming within inches of my already-injured leg.

I handed it back to Zarah. "Not for me."

She laughed and distanced herself. Weighing the end, she slipped the circle around one wrist and began to spin the chain. After getting a feel for it, she launched it at the throne. The dull back of the weapon hit the wood and bounced harmlessly away.

She shrugged. "I don't believe that's bad for a first try."

"No, certainly better than my attempt. Still, I'd keep it stored away for now and use your trusty sword instead."

She rolled up the chain and hung it from her belt. "Obviously a weapon designed for a more nimble and graceful warrior."

We ate a meager lunch and set out again. The rest of the floor contained more storage rooms and barracks. We backtracked to a path that split off from the main halls. It led to the familiar door that we'd seen on most of the previous levels.

I turned the key, revealing the path down. A blast of cold air caused me to involuntarily shiver. "Odd. The temperature should remain steady at this depth. If anything, it rises as you go deeper into the ground."

Zarah looked worried. "Perhaps we shouldn't go any farther. I sense something...unnatural."

"I wasn't aware you possessed psychic abilities. Why do you say that?"

"It's...just my intuition. There's something down there."

"We either go down or up. We know we can't defeat the arbolisk, so down is the most logical direction."

"Just...be careful," she said as she waited for me to enter the stairwell. Her change in demeanor was concerning.

We stepped down into the cold stairwell and began our descent toward whatever had unnerved her.

CHAPTER NINETEEN
Insurmountable

The temperature dropped as we descended. Our breath became visible by the time we reached the bottom. My leg protested the work I required of it. One thing was certain: if we camped on this level, it would be extremely uncomfortable due to the temperature. I hadn't expected it to change so abruptly.

"We should go back up and rest for the night," Zarah said.

"We can't afford to spend so much time resting. Our food will run out in the next few days. We have to find more resources or an exit before that happens."

The door led to a long hall. The stonework gleamed like obsidian. The floors, walls, and ceiling were perfectly square without an imperfection. As we followed the only path before us, the temperature continued to drop. After twenty minutes cautiously exploring, we reached the end of the passage.

There had been no rooms or branches from the hall. The doorway opened into a vast room of utter darkness. Directly across from us, a single speck of light dotted the blackness, like a sole star shining in the night's sky. The gargantuan room looked to be at least fifty times bigger than the church.

"What manner of place is this?" I asked.

"An unholy place," Zarah said, shivering.

Instead of heading directly toward the light, we opted to follow the left wall around. There was no telling what types of traps or other obstacles awaited in the vast, open space.

The walls, floors, and ceiling of the room matched those of the hall. We hit the left wall and continued around. Zarah studied the floors and walls, wary of traps. I cast detect magic several times, but it revealed nothing. After a while, we reached the far wall and began making our way directly toward the light.

It soon became apparent a low-burning torch was responsible for the room's illumination. As we drew closer, I could see a small alcove. Standing in front of the alcove a towering armored figure stood guard.

He was close to seven-foot tall and covered head-to-toe with heavy, black armor. His armor blended into the surrounding stone. It was as if the floor regurgitated a figure in the shape of a man. Two curved horns protruded from his helm. His hands rested on the crossguard of a large two-handed sword. The black blade pointed down, the tip resting on the floor.

Zarah and I looked at each other. I motioned for her to stand back while I approached.

"Hail!" I said as I moved cautiously closer. The warrior did not move. "Hail, friend!" I shouted. There was no reaction. Perhaps it was a statue. I inched closer and moved around so I could see the armor from the front.

The barbute-style helm contained a wedged slit for the man's eyes and an open slit that traveled downward at the center where the nose would be. I could see no hint of a figure inside, only darkness. Was the armor empty?

I returned to Zarah, unwilling to get any closer. "It seems to be empty. Perhaps it's a display or a trophy."

We moved around the wall, keeping our distance from the armor, and entered the alcove. The same type of door as the previous levels awaited us.

We searched the immediate area, but the key was absent. We eyed the armor.

"Stay here," I said as I moved closer to the ominous figure.

"What if it's trapped? You won't know what to look for."

"All right, but stay behind me," I said as I raised my shield and moved behind the towering immobile knight.

Suddenly, the head spun about to face us. Two glowing-blue eyes popped open. "Intruders," a deep voice said from within the armor. The voice echoed as if coming from within a cave.

The rest of the armor creaked and moaned as it turned to match the same direction the head now faced. The warrior easily hefted the massive sword and moved to strike.

"Get back!" I shouted to Zarah. She sidestepped away as I analyzed our opponent. I cast a detect magic spell. The blade glowed in a bright red aura, while a blue outline radiated out from the rest of the armor.

The warrior swung his sword toward me, but I leapt back. My injured leg warned me that I shouldn't depend on it. I could feel the wind from his blow, even at this distance. No human could wield a blade that large with such speed.

"We should retreat," Zarah said as she unwound the strange weapon she'd found on the floor above.

"If you wish to proceed, you must defeat me," the warrior said. An image of the key appeared in front of him for a brief moment before it faded.

"We have no quarrel with you. We merely wish to leave this place, great warrior," I said.

A deep laughter reverberated through the armor's thick metal. "All who come for punishment wish to leave. Remain still and I shall send you on your way." He took a step forward and readied another swing.

I backed up, keeping my distance. Our foe was obviously not human, which meant he could have any number of abilities. Zarah began to play her flute. I felt a surge of strength from her melody.

The armored warrior paused for a moment and regarded her as if seeing her for the first time. "You..."

Zarah's melodic tune stopped as she hit an impossibly loud, harsh note. Our opponent staggered for a second as if the music had caused him physical pain. "Such attacks have little effect on me."

I dove in and slashed at his arm, but the blade bounced harmlessly off. He brought his sword around just as I leveraged my shield to block it. The blow flipped my shield high into the air and sent me tumbling backward. I landed on my back fifteen feet away as the shield skidded across the floor. He approached, ready to swing again, but I rolled away until I was on my feet. Retrieving my shield, I noticed a large dent now adorned the front.

I ran forward but feinted just as he swung. Slashing at the joint behind his knee, I attempted to find a weak spot in his armor, but once again the blade did not penetrate. Despite

Zarah's song twisting and my ring, I felt as if I was barely moving faster than he was. Then I realized the temperature had continued to drop as we'd fought. The cold was hindering my movement, but it was a blessing as well — the pain in my leg had been numbed so my leaping and dodging were causing me minimal pain at the moment.

He brought his sword down in a wide, arcing stroke. For a split second, I considered blocking it with the shield but opted to dodge to the side instead. The maneuver probably saved the shield and my arm. The glistening stone floor erupted in rock chips and dust where the massive sword impacted it. A long crack ran from the tip of the blade for ten feet.

I then noticed a small gap in his armor near his lower back, where the breastplate and fauld connected.

We circled around each other. His blade had twice the reach of mine, but I was faster and more nimble than he was due to my lighter armor, enchanted ring, and Zarah's bard songs. But I needed a distraction.

"Ignatous Fragmentum!" I shouted as I pointed my hand at his face. The fiery dart surged forth and struck just below his helmet. He raised his hand to shield his face, only to find a summoned orb of light directly in his eyes. He lashed out with his sword, but I'd dashed in and slid on the ground, coming up beside him. I jammed the enchanted dagger with all of my might directly into the vulnerable spot. It sank into the armor, halfway up the blade. I rolled away before he could attack again. I could only hope the enchanted blade did some damage.

The armored warrior stiffened, as if in pain, but a deep laughter rumbled forth. He reached around, grabbed the dagger, and jerked it free. A white cloud of frozen mist trailed the dagger as he brought it around to study it.

"You think you know the cold? Cold is the icy grasp of death as the executioner's axe kisses the back of your neck on a winter's morn. This is a child's toy," he taunted as ice slowly covered the dagger. He crushed it in his massive gauntlet, letting the pieces clatter to the floor.

"We need to retreat!" Zarah shouted out. She looked as if she was tiring from her frenzied playing.

"It is too late for that," the armored warrior said. I readied myself and raised my sword and shield in a defensive posture.

"There is no defense for mortal fear," the warrior said as he grasped his helm in one giant hand while easily holding his massive two-handed blade in the other. He pulled off his helmet revealing...terror. My heart froze in my chest as all courage evaporated. Screaming, I ran for my life. The world became a blur as my only thought was, "Escape!" Rational thought had no place in this state of mind.

I came to my senses halfway up the steps to the previous level. I did not recall the run down the long corridor. Sweat stung my eyes as my heart felt as if it was going to vibrate apart. Our foe was a legendary death knight. Zarah was alone with a monstrosity.

I dashed back as fast as I was able, but paused halfway down the hall. We had no way of defeating the monster using our current combat methods. Physical attacks with normal weapons had no effect, and he was immune to cold. His armor seemed to be resistant to low-level magical attacks like my spell darts. Then an idea occurred to me. I set my sword on the ground and began drawing symbols. I had to hurry – Zarah needed me.

Long minutes later, I was done. Having caught my breath, I ran the remaining distance in a sprint, but I was limping by the time I reached the room. The numbness from the cold had worn off, and my damaged leg screamed at me to stop. When I arrived, Zarah was in a desperate battle with the knight.

"I will kill him," the knight hissed. "You can't protect him. You do not have the power. Not now."

"I'm your foe, death knight, not her," I said as I limped toward him.

He slowly turned. "Surprising. Most men are affected by my dread gaze for ten minutes or more. You did not even soil your pants."

I assumed a fighting stance and circled around him. He rested his sword on his shoulder and calmly waited.

Zarah backed away. She looked exhausted, as if she'd been fighting hard since I was driven off. "I have to rest a bit before I can play again. You're on your own for now."

I was still out of breath from the long run down the hall and across the massive room. The knight walked forward and brought his sword down at an angle. I deflected it with my sword, but the blow almost ripped it from my grasp. I couldn't absorb or parry a full blow from the giant sword.

"A word of caution: I do not tire. I do not sleep. My eternal duty is to guard that door."

"I'm to believe no one has ever made it by you?" I asked as I backpedaled. He did not follow. It seemed he would not travel a certain distance from the door.

He stood passively in silence. A fog of breath erupted from his helm, and his eyes glowed brighter. It seemed as if I'd angered him. "Certainly no one as weak as you." A wave of cold radiated from the spectral warrior. He turned his back in a deliberate act of contempt and walked back toward the door.

I dashed forward, ready to slide my full sword into the small open spot in his armor.

"Hero, no!" Zarah shouted.

Too late. I slipped and found myself sliding on my back toward the knight. He'd coated the gleaming floor with a sheet of ice, and I hadn't noticed. He turned and raised his blade high. I couldn't stop in time.

As the blade began its descent, Zarah's silver chain whipped around the tip of it, preventing it from moving. The warrior brought his large boot down upon my chest and pinned me to the ground. It felt as if someone had set a boulder directly on my sternum.

Reaching up, he grabbed the chain. In one motion, he jerked it toward him. Zarah tumbled forward, off balance.

"Die, and let it all die with you," the knight said as he reached out and touched Zarah's outstretched arm. She gasped as her skin turned pale and her flesh withered. It looked as if she'd lost a quarter of her body weight instantly. She tumbled to the ground beside me, blinking rapidly in surprise.

"No!" I shouted as I grasped the knight's ankle and pushed. It was like trying to move an iron pillar.

Zarah's voice was a raspy whisper. "Keep...fighting." The light faded from her eyes. Her skin became ashen.

"No!" I shouted again as I reached for her. Her body soon began crumbling to dust, leaving her belongings and clothing behind.

The knight reached down and grabbed me by my vest, lifting me up easily with one hand. "My death's touch. It's a painless, merciful death. She did not suffer. Unfortunately for you, I can use it but once a lunar cycle. However, you fought well, so I will merely freeze your heart as a sign of respect. Drift off to eternal slumber, brave fool."

Ice began to coat my vest where he touched it. I could feel my skin begin to freeze underneath my clothing. Suddenly, I became lightheaded and sleepy. I had no hope of beating this unearthly warrior from the grave. I closed my eyes and waited. At least my struggle was over.

Zarah's face flashed into my vision. "Keep...fighting." I thought of the suffering she'd endured, the trust she'd placed in me. My failure to protect her. I opened my eyes and clenched my teeth.

I brought my sword up and jabbed it directly into the opening in the death knight's helm. He did not flinch or react. In fact, I did not feel any resistance to the blade — the helm felt empty.

"One last desperate act of defiance. You've courage, I'll grant you that. But in this world, raw power is what matters, and you are sorely lacking," the knight said.

I slid the blade down, tilting it into the neck until half the blade was embedded in the empty armor. My hand crawled along the hilt of my sword until it found the pommel. A rune on my palm flared as a matching rune ignited on the blade. Fire erupted from inside the helm and through the gaps in the armor's neck and shoulders.

The knight dropped me to the ground and stumbled back as smoke billowed out from various spots in his armor. Coughing, he seemed to be in a daze as he asked, "What...?"

Again, I touched the summoning symbol on the sword's hilt. Another eruption ignited from within the dark warrior, this time slightly lower. He grabbed for the sword, but I activated the third summoning sigil on the sword's blade, launching another fiery dart into the interior of the suit.

The knight fell to his knees as his armor sizzled. He slammed his sword to the ground to steady himself and began to rise. The armor began to shake before he fell forward, face-first. The key slid away from his prone body.

I reached in and grabbed it, unsure if it was a trick. Smoke seeped out between the armor's joints.

I limped over to Zarah's body — nothing remained except her clothing, armor, and gear. I touched my finger to the dust and turned away before I remembered her treasured necklace. I sifted through the dust until I found it and looped it around my hand, squeezing it tight.

An emptiness and loneliness like none I'd ever known seeped into my soul. Could I make it on my own? Should I even attempt it? The dangers had grown the deeper we had gone until finally we'd met one that we could not overcome. At least not without an agonizing loss.

I then recalled the satchel, which held our supplies. I bent down to retrieve it. A flicker of light caught my eye. Zarah's flute reflected the nearby torchlight. I stored it in the satchel as a new resolute determination filled me. I'd escape this place or unravel its mystery for her.

Exhausted, I limped toward the door and opened it. Instead of a stairwell down, I was greeted with very short hallway. Magical orbs of red light illuminated the black obsidian-like stone. The hall ended in a large room which contained two giant doors. I paused, wondering what beast awaited me on the other side. Should I rest and recover my magic reserves, or forge ahead? Almost on cue, the double doors opened inward as if welcoming me. Cautiously I stepped forward, trying to see what dangers might be present.

The room appeared to be another throne room. On the far side, a solitary throne adorned a platform atop a raised dais. A series of steps that started wide and grew narrower led up to the dais, almost like a pyramid. A shrouded figure sat in the shadows, unmoving. Another long-dead conqueror? Perhaps one of the felae? I crept forward, warily looking for traps. I'd grown too reliant on Zarah's keen eyes.

To my left, a large, dark pool of liquid filled a perfectly circular fifteen-foot-wide basin in the floor. It was too dark to be sure, but it looked to be blood. A bath in the throne room?

I climbed the steps. The figure on the throne wore an arcane robe with its hood pulled up. Its bowed head faced down, shielding the figure's face in shadow. It held a magnificent staff across its lap. I was transfixed by it — I could feel its power without even casting a detect magic spell.

I reached out to touch it, when the robed figure looked up and spoke in a low, raspy voice, "Welcome."

CHAPTER TWENTY
Disciple

I leapt back, unsheathed my sword, and almost tumbled down the stairs.

"Careful. It would be a shame if you died from a broken back after all you've been through," the figure said. The lights in the room grew slightly brighter, allowing me a good look at the mysterious man's face. He was extremely old, almost skeletal. His gray, film-covered eyes flitted about. A large, curved beak-like nose dominated his face in an almost comical way.

"Not much to look at, am I?" He chuckled. "You should have seen me three hundred years ago. Surrounded by a harem of wenches, all trying to gain my favor by proving their prowess in new and imaginative ways." He sighed. "It's all gone now."

I eyed him warily, unsure of his motives. "Who are you, old one? What are you doing here?"

He smiled a toothless smile. "Who am I? Long ago, my name was feared for thousands of miles. They knew of me in Kodiva, halfway across the world. My name is Meister Orgun Mestaleze. Many called me the Angel of Suffering."

I'd heard the name before, but it was in a book of children's fables. "That would indeed make you several hundred years old, which is impossible."

Orgun shook his head. "Impossible is a concept developed by weak, lazy minds. Such talk is beneath you."

"You speak as if you know me. We've never met before," I said.

He laughed, but the laughter turned into a fit of coughing. His hand shook as he wiped the side of his mouth. "We've met once before, and I know you better than you know yourself. You see — I'm the one who stole your memories. They are all here." He pointed to the side of his head. "Well, to be more accurate, I have to remove the spells in your head that hold your memories. I hope you don't mind the fact that I perused them myself, so that I may study your past."

My anger flared for a moment before turning to confusion. "Why...how?"

"First, I must tell you a bit of this place. We must act quickly because I fear my time is approaching. This is a dungeon of power. One specifically designed to worship and feed Castigous, the God of Punishment. Over three centuries, thousands of people have been imprisoned, tortured, and killed here in the name of our master."

"Why does such a foul place exist?" I asked.

"Foul? Nay, this is a holy place. It exists to punish the guilty, the sick, the corrupt. Unfortunately for many, this includes most of mankind and other races. They are all guilty of one thing or another. After so long, you lose track of which one is at war with the other one, or which one hates the other based on if they have fur or green eyes. It doesn't really matter. Here, all are equal and receive adequate punishment for their sins."

"You kidnap them and torture them for their sins?" I asked.

Orgun stared away as if in a daze. He snapped back to reality after a moment. "No...well, occasionally. Our location precludes that method. No, we lure them here. Jewels, gold, artifacts, and...power. You've felt it and experienced it, yes? You've grown stronger as you've delved ever deeper. Your magic, your muscles, your mind. They've all improved as you've been tested?"

"Yes. I thought I was imagining it, but I couldn't deny it after several levels. I don't understand it."

He cleared his throat. "Here, in these places of power, you'll take part of it into yourself as you conquer the obstacles. It's possible to transcend human limits by traversing these locations."

"Why? What do you gain by allowing your foes to grow stronger?" I asked, genuinely curious. This was a topic I'd never explored or even heard of.

"Because once you defeat them, imprison them, torture them, you'll draw the power back from them, amplified. It feeds the dungeon. Think of it as nurturing a tree. You plant a seed, and with a little water, sunlight and nutrients, a mighty tree grows, providing fruit, wood, fire. The key is to chop it down before it becomes too large, else it crushes you."

"What is the purpose of it all? Why are you explaining this to me?" I asked, suddenly realizing I'd been conversing with someone whose dungeon had been trying to kill me.

"As I said, to punish the guilty. Think of it as a way to balance good and evil. Many of the world think they are good, yet their evil ways lead to the suffering of others. Many who are considered evil are merely performing necessary tasks that the weak find too distasteful. As for why I am telling you this: it's because I want you to do these things. I want you to mete out punishment. You are well-suited for it. Strong, intelligent, with a gift for magic. A rare breed, indeed."

I shook my head. "Why would you even think I'd ever work for you, torturing and maiming for an evil god? I merely wish to escape." With that last statement, I took a step forward and leveled my sword toward his neck. "You're going to tell me how to get out of this place..."

"Or you'll kill me?" he asked as he studied my face. "Yes...I believe you'd do it. You still seethe with anger over the loss of your companion."

I clenched my teeth at his mention of Zarah. "Speak her name and I'll gut you. I'm running out of patience, wizard."

He chuckled. "There's so much you don't know. What if I told you that you could bring her back?"

For a moment, I didn't know how to respond. "What? I'm no high priest or cleric. There's no coming back from being reduced to dust, even if I were. There must be at least a spark of life in a freshly dead body. No one can revive her."

"No...you can. You can use the power of this place to do so."

"I already told you I don't intend on becoming your servant."

"No, not a servant...you'll become the dungeon's master. You'll take my place. My time is almost at an end."

"Master? I don't..." I began to protest but thought about it for a moment. Perhaps I could accept his offer and use the power to escape. I then thought of Zarah's shocked expression as the life drained out of her. What if he was right about being able to bring her back? No, surely this was some trick.

"What do you gain out of it if I accept your offer?" I asked, attempting to discern his ulterior motives.

"Peace. I've suffered this place for years upon years. Wasting away due to my follies. The torturer has become the tortured. Perhaps a cruel irony visited upon me by Castigous himself. I've served him for many years, but his favor is fickle, and his punishments can be severe — even for his most loyal servants. I can't recover my power. There's nothing for me any —" he said before he began coughing again. A few flecks of red dotted his hand as it came away from his mouth.

"What is involved with accepting your offer? I merely wish to understand your terms and the consequences," I said. I had no idea if the old man was even who he claimed to be. For all I knew, he could be a devil or jinn in disguise, attempting to capture my soul.

"It's simple — you merely kill me."

The idea of killing a sickly old man seemed abhorrent. "How do I get out of this place? I have no interest in your bargain. Tell me, or I'll..."

"Do what? End my life? That's what I want. I'm unable to end my suffering myself. Castigous would torment me for eternity if I allowed one of his dungeons to collapse."

"One of them?" I asked.

He smiled. "You have no idea of the secrets that will unlock for you if you accept. The world you know is nothing compared to the dark knowledge you'd gain sitting on this throne."

"The world I know? I know nothing! You've torn my memories from me, and I demand them back!"

"Ah, yes. Perhaps that will be a better motivator than my offerings thus far," he said as he motioned for me to come closer.

I kept my sword between us as I drew closer. "No tricks. I don't know if you speak the truth, but I'll kill you at the first sign of deception."

He motioned for me to kneel in front of him. Leaning forward, he seemed as if he might collapse at any moment. His bony hands shook as he placed them on the sides of my head. "No deception. Only truth. Returning your memories will be severely taxing on me. It took a great deal of magic to block them while leaving you with your general knowledge. Don't resist me. Clear your mind."

I studied his face before staring him in the eyes. Closing my eyes, I waited for him to begin chanting or for some other indication he was performing a spell. Instead, the world fell out from under me, and I flailed into darkness.

CHAPTER TWENTY-ONE
Lost

I blinked several times as my eyes adjusted to the blinding light. I was outside! A wave of dizziness washed over me, and I reached out to steady myself.

"Hey, don't touch the merchandise!" a voice called out.

My eyes slowly focused on a large, fat man standing behind a cart. My hand was on a roll of fabric. Like the roar of an ocean, the sound of hundreds of people washed over me all at once. Looking around, I found myself in a marketplace.

"S-sorry," I said as I backed away from the merchant and almost bumped into a horse.

"Where?" I asked as I looked around. I then noticed I was wearing a hood pulled down over my face, and the need to stay hidden entered my consciousness. I ducked away from a guard and followed my instincts to head away from the crowd. It appeared to be twilight and the sun slowly fell from the sky, illuminating it in a pink and orange glow.

I entered an alley as the darkness grew. The sellers and artisans began packing up their wares to head home for the night. A few stragglers meandered about, but the marketplace emptied out fairly quickly. A handful of dogs rushed in to see what crumbs or tidbits they could find.

A sharp point jabbed into my lower back as a low voice whispered, "You know what I want. Give it to me."

Fear washed over me before my faded memory kicked in. "Oh, you're going to get it," I said as I whirled around and grabbed my assailant. She laughed and embraced me.

"Why do you insist on meeting in the city?" I asked.

"Because this is where the excitement is. You want to hide me away in the forests like some kind of lonely hermit."

I lifted back her hood to reveal her bronzed complexion and long, dark, wavy hair. Her beauty stunned me every time. "Yes, that's because our countries are still technically at war. Do you know what they'd do to you if they found you here?"

She drew in close and kissed me deeply. "I'm more interested in what *you're* going to do to me."

We left the alley and headed to an inn in the slums district. I tried to remember why we were meeting in such an establishment, but my memory was fuzzy.

We slipped into a dimly lit booth in the corner and ordered drinks. Aiyla's exposed leg rubbed against mine. "It's been too long since I last saw you."

I tried to recall our last meeting, but it was yet another memory that hadn't materialized. I stared into her deep brown eyes and felt as if I was falling into a well. "Are you sure you aren't using mesmerizing magics on me?"

She smiled. "Why? Is your mind more befuddled than it is normally?"

Each time she smiled, I felt as if I'd won some invaluable treasure. I glanced around the room. None of the women present were even fractionally as beautiful as Aiyla. Since meeting her, I knew of what all the bards in the world sang about when they offered their tributes to love and beauty.

After drinking and eating the best fare the establishment had to offer, we rented a room. Both of us laughing, we stumbled toward the stairs. The vulgar establishment faded away as Aiyla became my focus. We were all alone in our own world.

"Watch it!" a short, muscular man shouted from my side. He held a mug in his hand, and liquid ran down his shirt.

"My apologies," I said as I began to walk away.

"Where do you think yer goin'? You owe me a gold for messing up my shirt!" he said as he began to follow. I then noticed several men moved along with him. They looked like rough customers.

I looked to Aiyla for guidance. She shrugged. I reached for my coin purse and tugged the string.

"Oy, you got beer on my shirt too!" one of the other men said. The third one nodded in agreement.

I sobered up slightly as my adrenaline began to pump. These ruffians meant to shake us down. Once again, I looked to Aiyla. She nodded and put her hand on her hidden weapon.

I turned to the barkeep. "One round for these fellas, on me."

The three men nodded in agreement as they received their mugs. I began to edge away, but the short one looked up. "Ay, you ain't given me my gold yet." He slammed his mug on the bar.

"Sorry, I don't think that shirt's worth a gold. If you gave *me* a gold, I might go bury it far away so it won't stink up the room," I said. I cursed myself for saying it. Perhaps the alcohol had muddled my senses, allowing bravado to take over.

Aiyla shook her head as the three men dashed forward. Her whip caught the largest one directly in the nose, slicing it open. I blocked a punch from the next mugger as I brought up a kick that sent the small one tumbling into a table close by, turning it over. The men sitting there immediately grabbed the man and took turns punching him.

"I guess we'll have to find another place to spend the night," I said as we backed toward the door. Blast it, I'd just paid for the room here, yet we had to retreat due to these idiots.

"Aye, I've got a nice place for you to stay," a voice behind us boomed. We turned to find three heavily armed guards blocking the doorway. Aiyla looked at me with fear. What were they doing here? They normally patrolled the upper districts, not the slums.

"That's an interesting weapon you've got there, miss," the leader of the group said as he nodded toward Aiyla's whip.

"Reminds me of the ones those Nosteran bastards used on our soldiers during the last crusade." He pointed toward Aiyla and the other two guards seized her.

"Wait just a moment, we didn't start this fight," I said as I stepped forward. The captain reared back and punched me directly in the nose. I stumbled over a chair and fell on my back, stunned.

"My brother died in that crusade, so naturally I'm happy to take out my grief on Nosteran-sympathizers," he said as he strode forward and kicked me in the face. Aiyla screamed as the world faded away.

I AWOKE AS SEARING pain wracked the flesh of my back. I yelped involuntarily. As the scene came into view, I realized I was tied to a post. A crowd of hundreds of people was gathered around. Another crack of the lash caused the world to spin. I almost vomited.

"I...demand justice! Where is my trial!" I shouted as tears streamed down my face. The crowd laughed. How did I get here from the bar? Something was wrong. I couldn't remember.

A tall man in a long, black arbiter's robe meandered into my view. "You've had your day in court. You pleaded guilty. Do you not remember? The day you admitted to treason, all for the love of a foreign harlot? For shame."

I fought the pain and tried to remember, but it was gone. Agony split my back again. I felt warm liquid running down into my prisoner's trousers. I wasn't sure if it was sweat, blood, or urine.

A rock hit me in the forehead as a young man shouted something. All I could hear was the ringing in my ears.

"Where's...Aiyla?" I whispered.

"You'll find out soon enough," the arbiter said as pain overcame me.

MY BACK THROBBED AS I awoke. Trying to move, I found myself in a mobile stockade with my arms and head held in place and chains tying the mechanism to my feet.

Once again, a crowd of people had assembled, but this time I was in the midst of them, observing a platform in a courtyard. How much time had passed? A day? A month? Why couldn't I remember?

"This day, we are gathered to witness the execution of a foreign enemy who dared enter our fair city and attack our citizens. One of the heathen-born and godless Nosterans stands accused of these crimes," an arbiter in red robes shouted to the crowd. Massive booing ensued. He nodded in satisfaction.

"Yes, not only a Nosteran, but one of their foul wenches has infiltrated our city," the arbiter said as he judged the crowd's reaction.

I strained to see around him. To see who was on the platform. I prayed it wasn't Aiyla. He stepped aside and I cried out. She was bound to a block, her head bowed to the ground, unable or unwilling to look up at the crowd.

"Let her go!" I shouted. My throat was parched, and I found myself unable to raise my voice above the din of the bloodthirsty crowd. I jerked forward, but my chains were locked around something behind me. Turning, I could see they had been wound through two metal rings buried in the ground. A guard to my right noticed my struggle and hit the back of my leg with a metal rod. I refused to fall.

"On this ninety-first day of Dead Whisper, in the three-hundred-and-thirtieth year of our city's revival, we pray that Uxper guide our hand and shuffle this evil soul away from our righteous city!" the arbiter shouted.

The crowd murmured in agreement. The executioner stomped up the steps until he stood beside Aiyla. He held a large axe across his shoulder.

"What sayeth the people?" the arbiter shouted. The crowd booed and screamed, "Kill her," "Off with her head," and other vile things. I shouted for mercy, but no one heard.

"What sayeth the honorable king?" the arbiter shouted as he turned. I strained to look up, and for the first time noticed the king and queen sitting on a balcony, overlooking the proceedings.

The king extended his sideways-turned thumb and looked out over the crowd until his eyes settled on me.

"Show her mercy!" I shouted. My voice was nearly gone. I wasn't sure even the guards beside me heard my plea. I tried to let my eyes beg for her life.

He shook his head and frowned before turning his thumb down.

Again, I jerked my chains as I cried out. "Aiyla!" Despite the fact my voice had nearly given out, she looked up. It had been impossible for her to have heard me, but somehow, she found me. She smiled one last time before the axe fell.

Screaming, I jerked forward again. The crowd turned to regard me with a mix of sympathy and utter disgust. Now that the entertainment had concluded, they'd grown quiet. At last my voice was heard. "I'll kill you...I'll kill you all for this!" I shouted as I looked each one of them in the eye. "Even you!" I shouted up at the king. The queen covered her mouth in surprise. I couldn't tell if she was mocking me or if she was genuinely upset.

"She'd never done anyone any harm. She wanted no part of your war. She was good and beautiful. And you murdered her." My last sentence had dwindled to a whisper.

The red-robed arbiter stepped in front of me. "Silence this embarrassment." I lashed out, trying to grab the throat of the smug bastard, but the guard's club found my back first.

THE WORLD EXPLODED into view. I gasped for air as if I'd been submerged underwater for minutes. Reeling back, I fell down several stairs, knocking the wind from me. Groaning, I checked myself over before I climbed to my feet. Orgun sat on his throne, his face hidden in the shadows again.

"Take me back, dungeon master. You didn't finish the job. I need to know more!" I said as I climbed the last few steps. I was furious at what I'd just witnessed. Impotent anger and helpless sadness welled up within me. I'd known happiness once. True love. And my own carelessness had killed my Aiyla.

"Are you listening? I said fix my memory!" I said as I grabbed the wizard's shoulder. He toppled forward onto the floor.

"What..." I said as I turned him over. His lifeless eyes stared into oblivion. Blood soaked the front of his shirt and robe. I looked down at my sword. The tip glistened.

"No...no!" I whispered as I looked him over. I checked his pulse and breathing. His body was rapidly cooling. "No!" I shouted as I shook him. He'd returned only a few memories. Devastating memories that left me more confused and angrier than I thought possible. I wanted to strike out, to make someone pay for my agony. Instead, I was shaking an old man's corpse.

I was now completely alone again. Looking around the room, no door presented itself. There was no way out.

What now? Should I fight my way back to the top and assail myself against the door in the jail? I searched Orgun's body and throne but found no key. Surely he had a way to get out of his own dungeon? Perhaps with his death, the magic would fade. My sole desire was to return to that city and make the lot of them suffer.

Grabbing the staff, I inspected it. Perhaps there was a rune or spell upon it that could open a way out. After several minutes of poking, prodding, and using the few spells I knew, I gave up. If there was such an enchantment, it eluded my meager skills. I could feel the raw power within the staff but was unable to call it forth. It resisted an identify spell, which meant my power was too weak to draw out its true name.

I sat at the top of the steps and thought. My mind turned toward Aiyla. Her smile in the inn...her smile before she died. I had only two memories of her, but I knew there must have been many more. I was cheated of my freedom at the present and my memories of the past. The only logical way was forward.

I turned to descend the steps but cast one last glance over my shoulder at the wizard and his throne. No...my throne. I'd conquered the challenges that had been sent before me, and I'd earned my seat.

I turned and stepped over Orgun and rested myself on the large, ornate, wooden chair. It felt...good. Like it had been specifically created for me. I looked down at Orgun's frail form and tried to imagine him healthy and young. With the proper muscle and weight, he probably would have been similar to me in size.

Something caught my attention. I froze and listened. It had sounded like a faint whisper on the wind, yet no breeze blew through the room. "Back..."

I stood and surveyed the room. Had it been...Zarah? I shook my head. It felt as if I'd just lost two people close to me within minutes. In fact, they were the only two people I'd ever known, according to my incomplete memory. A crushing sense of loneliness overwhelmed me as I strode down the steps toward the pool.

I dipped one finger into the liquid and held it up to the orb of light. It wasn't as thick as blood, but the coloring and texture matched. Perhaps blood and water or another unknown liquid. I sat on the edge of the pool and let my thoughts drift away. My eyes became heavy as the battle and losses caught up to me.

The orb of light sputtered out. It seemed too early for it to expire, but I must have become lost in my thoughts for longer than I'd expected. A blue glow now illuminated the area. On the near wall, a large transparent sphere sat atop a pedestal that appeared to be sinewy arms overlapping and twisting around each other. At the top, five hands branched out from the center and grasped the mystical orb. In the bottom, a small puddle of glowing blue substance remained.

Had it been there before? I was sure I would have noticed it when I arrived, as it was directly within the line of sight of the entrance. Tentatively, I touched it, causing a low hum to emanate from the glass. It sounded crystalline in nature. "Bring me back."

I stepped away from the sphere, shocked. Looking around the room, I found no one else near, but I had definitely heard a voice – Zarah's voice.

Movement in the pool drew my gaze. It looked as if a single drop of liquid had disturbed the surface, but the ceiling appeared dry. Was I losing my mind? If not, I feared that I would soon.

Orgun had said it was possible to revive Zarah, but how? Without a body and a high-level holy man, that was impossible. Perhaps the rantings of a demented, lonely old man...

Again, something disturbed the pool. Focusing on the movement, an image of Zarah flashed in my mind. More concentric circles bobbed across the surface. I focused my will on the spot as rage bubbled within me. I thought of Zarah's face, her tale of suffering, the gentle way she'd mended my wounds and sang me to sleep. The center of the pool bubbled violently as if a school of hungry predator fish were feeding upon a hapless sheep that had fallen into a river.

"Zarah...return!" I shouted as I held out one hand toward the disturbance. A head broke the surface of the frothing liquid, but it was adorned with two curled horns and midnight-black hair.

"No, what...is this?" I said as I backed away. I reached for my sword, but I'd carelessly left it at the top of the dais. I turned to flee.

"Don't be afraid," a sultry voice said from behind me. I turned to see the figure slowly walking up out of the pool as if emerging from the depths of the ocean and coming ashore. The creature's body was that of a beautiful woman, but with a horned-skull, claw-like nails, and a thrashing tail. The crimson liquid glistened across her naked body as she approached me.

She stopped a few feet from me and smiled. "You did it."

"Z-Zarah?" I gasped.

She smiled, revealing predator-like fangs where her canine teeth should have been. "You don't recognize me, Hero?"

CHAPTER TWENTY-TWO
Decision

"There...have been some significant changes. How?" I said as I looked her up and down. Her face and body were the same, although she now possessed the bestial traits. As the liquid cascaded from her body, I noticed her skin tone had assumed a reddish hue — like that of a demoness.

"This is my true form. At least — the form the pool chose for me."

"What...when?" I asked. I felt like my brain was overflowing with stimuli.

"Just sit and rest. Let me explain."

I sat on the edge of the pool and reached out to touch her. My hand passed through her arm. Confused, I looked to her for an explanation.

"First...when I say this is my true form, this is merely a projection of my form. I don't have a true body. I am the core of this dungeon, a Dungeon Heart. You could say the dungeon is my body. I don't exist on the physical plane any longer. The liquid flowing around me inhabits both the physical and spiritual realms."

"But I touched you. You dressed my wounds."

"Let me start at the beginning — at least with your arrival. When you arrived in the dungeon, you were the first person to set foot here in over one hundred and fifty years. We're not sure how you entered because the entrance had caved in long ago. Perhaps the rocks have shifted recently, or you dug through. Of course, you wouldn't remember since Orgun stole away most of your memory."

"Can you return them? He's dead now," I said as I looked to the top of the dais.

A look of sorrow passed across Zarah's face. "Yes, I know. He was dying anyway. He maybe had months to live. The last few years had been agony for him...and me. As he grew weaker, so did I. The dungeon and the dungeon master are inextricably linked. I'm sorry...whatever blocks he placed in your mind can only be removed by his magic. In time, the barriers might break down naturally."

"What do I have to do with any of this?"

"When you first arrived, you were drunk and delirious. You screamed that you wanted to die. Orgun said you were suicidal. However, you were also our last hope. If you made it through the dungeon and were killed, we'd generate enough energy to continue surviving, and perhaps more adventurers would follow. The alternative outcome was that you killed Orgun, ending his suffering. You could then become the new master. He removed your memories but left you with your knowledge so that you could survive. If you wandered through the dungeon in the state in which you'd arrived, you would have died instantly, as you had no hope or will to live."

"You don't know who I was or anything else about me?"

"Orgun did. Once he gained your memories, he stated you were fated to come here, and that Castigous himself may have played a role in your arrival. He seemed very impressed with you."

"Why...did you pretend to be a prisoner? Why help me?"

"Orgun fell into a deep sleep after using the last bit of his magic to block your memories. He needed to recover. I took it upon myself to use a last bit of the dungeon's fading magic to assume a solid form — that of when I was human. I wanted to help in order to increase your chance of survival. It was...not a pleasant experience."

"And your own survival, too. If you know the dungeon so well, why weren't you of more help? How can I trust you are telling the truth?"

"The dungeon feeds upon the battles, magical combat, deaths, and torture of its guardians and challengers. Once the entrance closed decades ago, it fell into steady decline. Orgun placed me into a state of suspension to conserve magic until he awoke me upon your arrival. I was shocked at the state he was in and how the dungeon had fallen into disrepair. After a hundred and forty years of dormancy, my own memory of the dungeon had faded, and in my human guise, I had no control over the inhabitants or the dungeon itself. Despite being the Dungeon Heart, I'd lost most of my connection to the dungeon. Orgun's will works through me. I could no longer command the creatures in my incorporeal state without him. In fact, my magical reserves were completely depleted by that last act." She pointed toward the large sphere.

"That is the dungeon's life force...the Soul Sphere. It's also my life force. It was nearly empty before you arrived. Although the amount in it now seems small, it is more than it has had since the entrance collapsed. That came from our adventure through the dungeon. Overcoming the mysteries, your battles, your studies. All of your actions created this. With the death of Orgun, the dungeon switched its tether to you."

"I don't understand. Why would you think I'd want any part of this?"

Zarah walked to the Soul Sphere and caressed it while staring into its depths. "Because I wasn't ready to die or to allow the dungeon to die. The dungeon needs a new master, and you've earned that title. As you desired to throw your life away, this way it will serve a greater purpose. We made that decision for you. I'm sorry if it's not the outcome you sought."

"And if I wish to leave?"

She looked up at me, her alluring features illuminated by the soft blue glow of the orb. "You...can't leave. You would die, just as I would. If you left, you'd grow weaker the farther you traveled from the dungeon. In short order, you'd pass away. The dungeon's energy would collapse, and I'd cease to exist."

I stood and paced around the pool. "What good is this power? Trapped deep beneath the ground, unable to see the world ever again? A lord of rock, shadows, and misery? Why would anyone want such a life?"

Zarah disappeared from the Soul Sphere's side and reappeared in front of me. "You called out a name before you stabbed Orgun — Aiyla. Who was she?"

The fresh torment of those few memories rushed into my mind. "Someone...I loved very much. More than life itself. Orgun only returned a few memories. He must have started with my most intense or recent encounters. She was executed."

"I understand. Do you want vengeance against those who wronged you? You heard my tale. That's why I agreed to serve Orgun and the dungeon. To punish the wicked and greedy. The powerful and rich who masquerade as benefactors. The corrupt soldiers and supposed officers of the law who prey upon the weak. The falsely pious clergy who control the population by using religion and hopes while enriching themselves. There is no court of law who can hold them accountable, but the dungeon can."

I chuckled. "What good is a dungeon against those like King...blast it, I can't even recall the name of the current king."

"Because all evil and corrupt men seek power, money, and fame at the expense of everything else. While we can't attack the clergy and royalty directly, we can draw in their champions. We can erode their power, even from here."

"With what? A few baubles?"

Zarah smiled before waving her hand toward a far wall. A section of the wall disappeared, revealing an open chest of gold and gems, along with several weapons and pieces of armor stacked against the wall. Many of the smaller kingdoms probably did not have such wealth. "We have our ways of luring in our enemies."

I thought about Aiyla's last moments. The jeering crowds, the king, the guards, the haughty arbiters. At the moment, I'd have given anything to make them pay. Now...perhaps I had the tools. Turning from Zarah, I walked up the steps to the throne and sat. She reappeared beside me but remained silent.

"We'll need strong warriors," I said as I began to think through various strategies.

The sound of clanking armor, clattering, scratching claws, and shuffling caused me to shift my gaze to the entrance. In walked the death knight, followed by a large batch of goblins, skeletons, and two ratzgor. There must have been hidden passages on several levels that I hadn't located. The wraith that had possessed Emlee descended from the ceiling and stood beside the knight. To my surprise, the pig-man from the torture chamber brought up the rear of the motley group. To see so many enemies gathered at once caused my heart to skip a beat. I looked up at Zarah, but she smiled knowingly.

The small crowd stopped at the base of the steps and looked up at me before kneeling and holding their collective gaze to the ground. They shouted in unison, "All hail the Master!" They remained docile and unmoving as if awaiting instruction.

"What are your orders, Master?" Zarah asked.

"Now? Now we rebuild," I answered.

Author's Notes:

Please leave a review!
For the love of all that is holy, help a soul out!
[Join the Mailing List](1)
(Book release dates, exclusive deals, free book)
[Contact/Follow](2)

Other Books by S Mays:
https://www.s-mays.com/the-good-stuff.html

---

1. https://www.subscribepage.com/SMaysSuperbTales
2. http://www.s-mays.com/contact.html

Printed in Great Britain
by Amazon